Just Under the Sky is unlike anything I've read before, while also incorporating some elements from other notable works of fiction that I love. This novella is utterly enchanting and will keep you reading until you have finished the book in its entirety. R.K. is absolutely a break-out author and is very talented.

—Christie Jok

From the first page I was completely immersed in the text. Gold did an amazing job of creating a completely new world, and despite creating some fantastic and supernatural elements, he managed to make it believable.

—IDKtheEmcee

Just Under the Sky

R. K. Gold

Just Under the Sky

R. K. Gold

Weasel Press
Hitching for Words

Just Under the Sky
R. K. Gold

2016 R. K. Gold

ISBN-13: 978-0-9972968-1-5
Library of Congress Number: 2015940303

Publisher: Weasel Press
Manvel, TX
www.weaselpress.com

Printed in the U.S.A.

Distributor: IngramSpark

2nd Printing

Interior: Weasel
Garamond, 12pt

Table of Contents

JUST UNDER THE SKY

I

For the first time in almost a decade, someone made a break for the forest. What used to be considered youthful mischief was now punished as a severe crime. And the cheers from neighbors only made matters worse.

Jasper, a short, plump man who made a habit of hibernating in the bar, finished his latest article on Senior Elder McMichaels' verdict: Spencer would be forced back into field for the rest of his life. Jasper reclined in his wooden chair and sipped a cup of colni tea. He doubted Spencer would even be allowed to sleep in a bed again. The article ran next to the latest announcement by the Elder

Council: "The diminishing food supply has been a cyclical event that will correct itself without intervention," they confidently repeated every time the question was raised. Sometimes, when Jasper sat alone in the printing house, he would doodle a mustache on pictures of members of the Elder Council. As he buried his pen into a scrap portrait of Senior Elder McMichaels, Jasper noticed an article, by his coworker Judy, praising the Elder's latest precautions against a forest attack.

He rolled his eyes at the headline. As if the trees were actually going to uproot and charge their cottages. The fact that Jasper actually saw families reading these stories and praising the Elders made him fantasize about what life would be like beyond the forest.

Most of the village viewed Senior Elder McMichaels as a savior. He rose through the ranks of leadership during a time of turmoil. Ten years ago, he ended the food riots before they began by giving the people a common enemy; one that had haunted their mythologies since their ancestors originally settled.

Being one of the only villagers ever to wander into forest's depths, the Senior Elder claimed the folklore was true; the forest was home to a creature of pure evil; it was a creature that wanted nothing more than to punish those it could; and the forest would claim the life of anyone who spent three days within its boundaries.

Most of the villagers spent their entire life without even imagining what lay on the other side of the threshold. They believed every syllable the Senior Elder spoke and went about their days.

Though the Elder Council had convinced most villagers that the food shortage would fix itself, a growing minority remained silently skeptical. For the first time in Jasper's life, he had actually heard groups of people flirting with the possibility of deserting. However, those flirtations were quickly dismissed. Peace in the village was waivered on a daily basis, and no villager wanted to be the spark that melted the glue.

And even those who wanted to escape through the forest believed the stories. No one knew exactly what awaited travelers who wandered within its grasp.

McMichaels Jr. drummed on Jasper's desk with his knuckles. "How's the praise of the all knowing and all powerful going?" His dark red curls bounced over his face.

"Could be better." Jasper took a long sip of tea and leaned forward, resting his elbows on his desk. "How's living with the all knowing and all powerful?"

An arrogant smirk broke across McMichaels' face like thin ice under the pressure of a rhino. "As typical as ever. Actually, I think it's more typical now."

"Care to explain?" Jasper poured a second mug for McMichaels and slid it across his desk. He always had two ceramic mugs in his drawer, and McMichaels returned the favor. The end of day rants in the privacy of the abandoned printing house had been a growing tradition since they both began working at the press.

"He's planning another crusade against the forest. Acting as if the trees on the edge are some sort of dangerous spies that must be destroyed. Everyone will love him for it and think he is a brave and brilliant man but, let's be honest, they're just trees."

"I can't argue with you there. They are trees."

McMichaels looked at Jasper skeptically over the brim of his mug. "Alright Jasp, how bout you tell me what's on your mind. I can see a half baked idea melting out of your nostrils. It's kinda gross."

"No, it's nothing," Jasper said, tapping his mug. "I've just been feeling a little claustrophobic lately."

"Need to go for a walk?" McMichaels stood up from the desk.

Jasper paused for a moment. He felt the warmth of his tea fill his chest and stomach and wanted nothing more than to bathe in the sensation for as long as possible. But he could feel a building pressure below his stomach that would have to be relieved soon. "No, I'm alright," Jasper gestured for McMichaels to stay seated. "It just would be nice to see what else is out there."

There was another long moment of silence. Both men seemed desperate to end it but it was as difficult as speaking through a vacuum. Jasper knew he had crossed a line. The Elders had spies everywhere and were looking for any excuse to sentence someone to field labor: One less mouth on village rations and two more hands collecting food.

He handed McMichaels the article on his father. "I think I got everything. Well, I know I got everything since there is nothing to actually say. But I need at least a second opinion, and then a second opinion for that opinion so take it."

The atmosphere lightened immediately and the two men finished their tea. Jasper poured them each a second cup and walked towards the back exit. McMichaels followed and the two of them laughed as they found a private place to relieve themselves.

"I think I know what you need," McMichaels said, pulling up his trousers.

"Oh yeah? What's that?" Jasper wiped his hands on McMichaels' white button down shirt. McMichaels brushed his hands away and jokingly cocked a fist.

"A drink," McMichaels replied and started walking

down the cobblestone path toward the center of the village. They walked past the bakery where Jasper used to work. It was his first inner ring, job before McMichaels found him an opening at the printing house.

Most of the houses in the inner ring looked identical; they were small wood huts with a stone chimney.

"Remember when we used to sneak bread out to the forest and looked for the demon?" Jasper grinned.

"I remember you being too scared once the sun completely set," McMichaels replied. They walked past the village garden where the Elders spent most of their days studying. Four stone statues guarded the garden. They were supposed to be dedicated to the founders of the village, but Jasper always had trouble believing that.

"I thought the point of this place was to escape the corruption of worship in the outside world," he muttered to McMichaels as they both spit at the feet of the statues.

"I mean, the world beyond the forest destroyed itself long ago."

"Do you really believe that though?"

"Why wouldn't I? Why else would our people choose to live next door to a forest that's supposedly trying to kill us?" McMichaels replied.

"Maybe you have a point," Jasper answered. He almost bumped into a homebuilder. The man was wiping sweat off his face and was covered in dirt. He glared at Jasper for a moment and continued walking towards the outskirts of the village. They followed him a short distance and past the low wooden wall dividing the inner ring with the center of the village. Most of the buildings were still wood but they had far fewer windows and most of them did not have chimneys. As they walked closer to the edge, the houses continued to change. Some of them became a combination of mud and stone.

They finally arrived at Cheap Mind, the village's only social bar. "First couple rounds are on me, big guy." He ruffled Jasper's already messy brown hair before handing him a pint.

The bar seemed more crowded than it actually was. After walking past the first wall of people, the numbers spread out. They found two empty stools at the end of the bar and began to relax.

"McMichaels!" a high pitch voice sliced through the ambient murmurs.

Jasper and McMichaels both looked up and saw the wide brown eyes of their coworker Judy racing towards them. She smiled and adjusted her glasses as she side shuffled through the crowd. Judy was a new journalist at the Carousal and when she was not studying the history of the village, she was asking McMichaels about his father.

"So is it true that his lineage goes all the way back to the original settlers?" Judy poked McMichaels' shoulder so hard that he nearly spilled his drink. McMichaels rolled his eyes at Jasper, who chuckled and finished his drink quickly before Judy had the chance to clumsily bump into him. She was referencing a story that Jasper had rushed out almost a week ago after their editor insisted on beefing up the story a little more.

"I think," McMichaels said halfheartedly.

"I heard he is a descendant of the stars. Two of the village's greatest minds fell in love in the afterlife and sent him down here as a gift," Jasper said with a surprisingly straight face.

McMichaels' face turned red with desperately contained laughter. Judy turned to Jasper with an eager, white smile. If it were not for her obsessive attitude, Jasper may have found her attractive.

"Really? Who told you that?" Judy asked.

"Oh, the Moon and the Sun," Jasper replied as he reached for his second drink. It always surprised him when someone actually believed the village's greatest minds descended from the sky; but what else would he expect from a group of people that believed a forest was the birthplace of a local demon. McMichaels reached around Judy's back and paid for Jasper's drink.

"Wow! And you must be so overwhelmed. I mean having to live with such a great man. Do you ever feel stressed or nervous living up to his name?" Judy asked McMichaels.

McMichaels calmed down a bit and took a long sip from his glass. He stopped smiling and stared blankly at his drink. Jasper tried to catch his eye and see if he was alright.

"Hey Judy, maybe you could do us a favor?" Jasper asked, trying to get her attention.

"Depends on what it is," she replied keeping her gaze fixed on McMichaels.

"If you do it we can get you a one on one with the Senior Elder," Jasper said. Before he even finished Judy had jumped to his lap. The back of her legs pressed against his inner thigh.

"Could you run back to the office and grab a couple of the pink flowers in my top drawer?" Jasper asked. "They're right next to my ink."

"What do you need those for?"

"To drink."

"Sure!" Judy eagerly ran towards the exit. As Jasper turned back to check on McMichaels he heard her light, yet somehow loud, footsteps running back towards him. "Where's your desk?" she asked, almost bouncing in place.

"The corner window. Right next to the press."

And with that Judy was off. Jasper made sure she left the bar before turning back to his friend. "You hanging in there?"

McMichaels half nodded.

"If it makes you feel any better," Jasper began, "I got nothin'."

McMichaels' smirk was short-lived. "Come on, next one is on me," Jasper said before he downed his drink.

"No, it's okay. I think I might just call it an early night," he said finishing his pint and walking towards the door.

"Oh, come on man," Jasper grabbed his shoulder. "Look, you're," he pulled McMichaels in close enough to whisper. "Everyone loves your father. But since when have you let anyone else dictate your life? If you really want everyone to love you just start saying the forest is getting ready to attack or some crazy theory about its magic."

McMichaels didn't seem happy, but he did return to his seat. Denise, the youngest bartender came over to them and winked at McMichaels. "On the house," she said, pouring them both a full glass.

Judy returned with a handful of Colni flowers and eagerly gave them to Jasper. "I didn't know how many you wanted!" she said, shoving them into his stomach.

"Thanks, this is perfect." He put one flower in

his drink and mixed it with his pinky. He handed one to McMichaels and pocketed the rest. "You want to try one?" He plucked a petal and handed it to Judy. "Roll it up and push it between your lip and gums."

"By your back molar," McMichaels added.

"What is it?" Judy asked, holding the pink flower gingerly between two fingers.

"A Colni flower. You can only get it in the forest." McMichaels said, clinking glasses with Jasper.

Judy threw the flower at Jasper as if it were a stick of lit dynamite. "Don't hand me that toxin."

"Toxin? No, no, it's not poisonous. They sell it in the market. We've been drinking it for years." He held it up as if to demonstrate its harmlessness.

"Then you're toxic too! Don't you know how evil that place is?"

The bar quieted down. All eyes were on Judy, who seemed to relish the attention. She seized the flower from Jasper and raised it over her head for everyone to see. "The forest is pure evil. There is no good from such a place. As the Elder McMichaels always says, the stars are in the heavens, and the forest only obstructs your view." She tore the flower into small pieces and threw them to the floor. Everyone in the bar cheered her on. Judy smiled and waved, savoring the celebration.

McMichaels quickly rose from his seat and Jasper could see he was beginning to get a little hot headed. He wasn't the tallest man but still towered over Judy. Normally she would quiver in his presence but the background murmurs and cheers seemed to give her some newfound strength that Jasper had never seen. She pushed her chest out so it brushed against McMichaels' stomach and met his gaze. The two squared off with growing tension, set to explode any moment. Jasper could not look away

The two of them shuffled even closer; their noses were only inches apart. Jasper clung to his empty glass like a crutch, as the bar only grew louder. People began insulting Jasper and McMichaels:

"Evil!"

"Rot in Hell!"

"We don't want you here!"

The mob had actually morphed together into a single living body and spoke as one. Judy would not dare to throw a punch but one of the field workers, jealous of McMichaels' status and inner village job, might be a bit more reckless. Especially since Judy had already displayed an unusual amount of bravado. Normally she would be honored to pick up breadcrumbs around McMichaels' desk. If she were willing to push him around, what would the others be willing to do?

Jasper's fears sparked into action; Skid, a man built like a cannonball with a receding hairline, broke from the crowd and lowered his shoulder towards McMichaels. Working in the sun all day had left his skin dark and cracked.

McMichaels turned just in time and managed to duck just out of the way; the blow glanced the top of his head instead of knocking him out. Judy's earlier confidence flushed from her face and took all the color in her cheeks with it. She stood pale and frightened in the center of the bar as the focus shifted to McMichaels and Skid.

Skid threw another hook, but this time McMichaels easily dodged. He shoved his attacker out of the way and made for the exit, but the mob of people blocked his path. Most of them made rude gestures and swore at McMichaels, but some looked ready to join and tried to take a couple swings themselves.

Skid lowered his shoulder again and charged at McMichaels. He wrapped his arms around his waist and drove him through one of the tables. The crowd cheered; it was not a fight as much as a sport.

Jasper, completely unsure what to do, walked over to the debris. He saw Skid on top of McMichaels ready to swing at his defenseless face. Without a moment of hesitation Jasper swung at his head; what took him by surprise was the fact that he was still holding his pint. The glass smashed against Skid's temple. He fell to the floor beside McMichaels, grasping at the blow, trying to cover it with his hands. A few people from the crowd ran over to help, but most of the bar seemed more interested in retaliating. Jasper could feel their eyes burning through him. They weren't interested in sport anymore; they wanted murder.

He wouldn't be able to fight them all off. Especially with McMichaels still lying almost unconscious on the floor.

The mob slowly stepped closer and closer to Jasper. He was finding it more and more difficult to breathe. His vision blurred.

But a loud crash broke everyone's attention away from Jasper. There was a moment of relief; Jasper did not realize he was holding his breath until the pressure in his chest eased and he began gasping for air. The blurred crowd parted and admitted the sight of a figure walking toward Jasper. His eyes adjusted, and he could make out a tall man with a round gut, long, curly, grey hair and bushy mustache.

Senior Elder McMichaels had arrived. But why? Jasper looked over at McMichaels Jr. He was sitting up, rubbing the back of his head with a terrible look of embarrassment on his face. Though he and his father rarely saw eye to eye, they were good at hiding it in public.

"What appears to be the problem here?" the Senior Elder asked, looking around at the debris. Clearly he knew what happened, but most of the villagers were either too nervous or too awestruck to speak to him unless he asked a question they absolutely knew how to answer.

Judy stepped out of the crowd, adjusting her glasses. Some of the color had returned to her cheeks, but she still looked a little flustered.

She pointed to Jasper, and with a surprisingly authoritative voice said, "He and your son brought artifacts from the forest into the village." Everyone in the bar murmured approval. A few people even clapped. She was regaining her composure now and cleared her throat. Jasper had trouble not responding. How could she be so ignorant? Most of the medicine they used in the village came from the outskirts of the forest. And during food shortages, teams would go into the forest to collect whatever they could find.

"They tried to force me to consume something they had smuggled into the village and when I refused they became violent." Again the bar cheered, this time a little louder. McMichaels sat quietly with his back against the wall.

Judy seemed to relish the attention again and tried to drag out the account for as long as possible. Finally, Senior Elder McMichaels raised his hand and she immediately stopped. He took a moment, waiting for every last person to stop talking. "I applaud your enthusiasm to fight against such an evil. It is most admirable." Everyone seemed grateful for his approval. They all nodded their heads along and whispered excitedly to one another. "We have proven time and time again to be beings of supreme intellect. And I am both proud and grateful to consider each and every one of you my neighbor."

Jasper tried not to roll his eyes. He had heard the Senior Elder talk at great length about the simple-mindedness of the villagers. But he needed to ease the situation and flattery was one short cut that almost always worked. By now he had probably figured out what actually happened.

"But, living as a higher being comes with certain expectations." He crossed the room and helped Jasper to his feet. "If we resort to this kind of senseless violence in our pursuit of justice, then we become no better than what lives out there," he pointed outside. "The forest is a place of evil, and misery. Logic does not guide it, only survival." The bar remained silent in anticipation for what the Senior Elder would say next.

"But the other difference between us and them is our ability to admit when we are wrong," the Senior Elder continued. He walked over to McMichaels and helped him to his feet. Jasper could tell McMichaels was reluctant but he hid it well. "I want you two to apologize," the Senior Elder folded his arms. It was embarrassing. He was treating them like a parent would handle a five year old. Judy's smile almost grew too wide for her face. Jasper wished he could throw her in the forest and watch her smile die. He wouldn't have to take her far; in fact, she would probably faint if she just touched the threshold.

McMichaels did not put up much of a fight with his father. He knew he had to get it over with as quickly as possible and worry about the stinging pain later. "I apologize for being so very wrong," he said, and even through gritted teeth, he managed to sound almost sincere.

Jasper found it easier to apologize following McMichaels' lead. After their apologies, the Senior Elder extended his hand and made Jasper and McMichaels kneel before him. Jasper wanted to raise the irony that the metal used to make the ring came from the forest, but he remained silent, and killed time by looking at the deep spiral grooves on the ring's face.

The crowd seemed pleased and almost began to celebrate as if they had just accomplished some great victory. Judy seemed more interested in getting the Senior Elder McMichaels to notice her.

After deescalating the situation, the Senior Elder seemed ready to leave. He shook a few hands and congratulated everyone on their ability to handle the conflict. He then led McMichaels to a corner. Jasper couldn't make out a word; the sheer force of their personalities schooled their features into calmness, but he assumed they would clash upon returning home. Everyone at the bar seemed too pleased with themselves to notice.

Jasper and McMichaels found their seats back at the bar and were relieved to be left alone. McMichaels looked around the room and for the first time let his disgust noticeably surfaced. He ordered four pints and handed two to Jasper without even looking in his direction. "We're gonna need you to fill these up whenever you see that we're almost empty," McMichaels said, leaning over the bar and sliding a little extra money into the Denise's front pocket.

II

On a somewhat sunny day, rays of light just managed to find their way through the dense ceiling of the forest. A thick mattress of leaves coated the ground.

Rolling in his sleep, Jasper felt something dig into his side, pressing under his jacket. The stabbing pain forced him to his feet. The leaves crinkled under his weight, but Jasper didn't seem to notice. His eyes remained half closed as he crouched down to look for a comfortable place to fall back asleep. Jasper walked in a circle like a dog before dropping to the ground and curling up into a ball. As he began drifting back to sleep, something crawled over his knuckle. As if being simultaneously branded and struck by lightning, Jasper scrambled to his feet and ran blindly until the trunk of a thick tree halted his path. An overwhelming sensation of confusion and fear took hold as Jasper's eyes began to adjust to his surroundings.

In front of him, a monstrous oak stood at least a hundred feet tall. It glared down at him like he was an unwanted guest at a dinner party who had long overstayed his welcome.

"What the?" Jasper whispered to himself as he attempted to ease the stiffness in his neck. He looked side to side for any answer that would graciously climb down to him.

For a moment Jasper wondered if going back to sleep was the best idea. If he closed his eyes perhaps he would wake up in the comfort of his own bed. The idea certainly tempted him.

A deep hoot startled him away from his wishful thinking. There was something very different about this tree; it had cold, sharp bark. Much different than the trees Jasper climbed when he was a kid. He and McMichaels used to race to the top of the trees along the edge of the forest. Loser had to pick the Colni flower for their tea.

Though Jasper could not see much of the sun, he could tell that it was at least midday; light pierced through the leaves directly overhead.

Despite being lost, Jasper was thankful for the buffer between him and what he could only imagine was a clear blue sky. The thought of staring into even a dim light bulb made him shudder as he attempted to massage his headache away. He struggled to keep his eyes at a steady squint. Still convinced that he was just wandering through a dreamscape and at any moment would wake up, Jasper walked around the tree. He half expected to find a lever or something that would open up a hidden door to reality. But he gave up on this hypothesis after the third lap. Roots climbed out of the ground like uneven stairs.

Though the trees were dense, Japser still had more than enough room to fully extend his arms and legs. The ground, where branches weren't protruding, was covered in a dark brown earth and different colored leaves, which scratched against the bottom of Jasper's feet.

He was ready to force himself to wake up. Starting small, he pinched his cheek, but he could barely feel a thing. He then tried his neck but again there was no sensation. Finally, digging his nails into his arm, Jasper felt a small sting, but it was still not enough to wake him.

A twig lay directly in front of him; Jasper just wiped it clean with his baggy shirt. He poked at his arms, legs and stomach but still nothing happened. The stale atmosphere from the forest began to clog Jasper's nose.

31

He found it more and more difficult to breathe the thick, warm air. His breath quickened and shallowed. He needed to wake up now. Breaking the twig under his foot, he jabbed the jagged tip against the back of his leg; stabbing again and again until he was out of breath. Jasper pulled the twig away. It was tipped red and a warm fluid slid along the back of his thigh. He wiped his finger against it, and even though he was expecting blood, its warmth took him by surprise.

"This can't be happening," Jasper said, running around another tree looking for any exit he could find. But there was nothing. He did not care which way home lay; Jasper began to run. He ran, and ran, passing by tree after tree, looking for any opening that looked new or any opportunity to escape. He was exhausted, he could scarcely breathe, and after losing focus for just one moment, Jasper ran his shoulder full force into the trunk of a towering oak. All he could think about was the forest sucking the life out of him. He was always told that after three days the forest would completely drain any intruder. And now Jasper feared he was trapped in a death sentence; looking up at the dirt piling on top of him and trying to scream for help through an ocean of trees.

He fell to the ground hard, but couldn't relax. Every muscle in his body tightened and cramped as he looked up at the sky. All he could see were sporadic slivers of light mocking his incarceration. Sweat beaded his forehead, and without a breeze to blow it away, it stuck to his skin. But the air became more tolerable and his body seemed to be getting used to it. Slowly, he strengthened his breaths and filled his lungs instead of spitting the air out like salt water.

He was going to die. In three days would there be anything left of him? Did the trees leave behind a corpse or did they claim the entire body? Jasper desperately looked around for answers but could not see past his asphyxiation. He was trapped on his stomach with an unknown force pushing down on his back. The air felt like melting wax in his mouth. Jasper dug his fingers into the cool dirt, hoping for some sort of miracle as he descended closer to six feet.

His stomach cramped violently, stabbing at his sides. He assumed the pain came from the forest, the way it was eating away at him. For all he knew, he had slept through the first two days and awakened just in time to die.

What was he always taught about the forest? Jasper tried to rattle his mind but he had trouble focusing on anything except the lack of space. He could feel the trees moving closer together; and soon they would squeeze the life out of him. He might as well have been buried in the cemetery; at least then people would know where to find him.

The pressure building in his stomach became too much and over flowed. Jasper crawled on to his hands and knees and spat up everything he could. The thin fluid soaked into the ground almost instantly and vanished into the dirt. Was this what was to become of him? Would he be consumed too?

His throat and nostrils burned. The joints in his knuckles and wrists cracked as he pushed himself to his feet and he twisted his back side to side, feeling a couple large pops.

What had he always been taught about the forest? He rattled his brain but the answers lingered just out of reach. "Come on, think," he muttered to himself. "The forest was evil," Jasper muttered under his breath. That lesson was obvious and repeated at least a hundred times on a daily basis. "Come on, what else," Jasper repeated, still struggling to reach the rest of his memories. "A person is to never, to never," Jasper grunted impatiently. "Never wander within its depths," he finally managed to string the sentence together, but when he looked back at his surroundings he wondered how it would help him.

"And the forest will take my life in three days," Jasper added. The reminder sent chills down his spine. Suddenly, the quiet void he thought he wandered into began to stir. Branches snapped only a few feet away and little paws pranced over the leaves; Jasper could hear them crackling all around. He desperately searched for any sign of life; Jasper could feel his eyes widen and his pulse quicken. As his senses heightened, his memory clicked.

He had to move downhill. The Village was built at the lowest point of any nearby land. Their pond connected to the base of the mountains; snow constantly covered the mountains, and as the snow in the lower portions melted, streams of water flowed together into the pond. So as long as a person walked downhill, they were heading in the right direction.

After a long moment, Jasper found the strength to stand up. He still half-hoped he would wake from this nightmare. But as it became easier to breathe and the burning sensation in his throat diminished, Jasper found the confidence to take the first steps forward.

As he began the descent, Jasper found it difficult to keep his footing. He was off balance the entire time. Leaning against a tree for support, Jasper attempted to massage the burning sensation out of his legs. They trembled from the short hike.

"How did this even happen?" Jasper asked, and rubbed the back of his head. The forest almost absorbed the sound of his voice, leaving neither resonance nor echo.

The last thing Jasper remembered was sitting with McMichaels at the bar attempting to sober up. McMichaels was going on about his tense conversation with his father:

***

"Can you believe it? He says we need to have a serious discussion. About what? She's the one who decided to turn everything into a theater performance." McMichaels pointed to Judy who was still attempting to be the center of attention. She was reenacting her bravery for destroying the flower and while onlookers prompted her to continue.

***

However, after that conversation, Jasper's memory failed him. Did he and McMichaels go out to the forest together? Even in a belligerent state Jasper believed he would not be stupid enough to do so. Jasper cringed as he thought about what would have happened if he they were caught. Nevertheless, that fear felt more like a blessing as Jasper glanced at his surroundings. "Why weren't we caught?"

"McMichaels!" Jasper shouted. There was a long and exhausting moment of silence that seemed to weigh on Jasper's shoulders. Again, the sound of his voice disappeared into the forest. He was eager to break the silence again, but before he could repeat his cry, he heard a crack over his head.

A hissing sound followed immediately after. Jasper cautiously looked up. He did not want to make any sudden movements. Looking for the animal that made the noise, he clenched his fists and gazed around the tree. As he tried to convince himself it was all in his head, the hiss sounded again. Desperate to find the source, he spun in place, scanning his surroundings. Jasper's legs were trembling. He was holding on to the nearest tree when he spotted something. Perched on a branch maybe ten feet off the ground sat a small fur ball of a creature. It held something close to its chest. Jasper realized he was being threatened by a squirrel.

A huge wave of relief splashed over Jasper. He walked over to the base of the tree, holding his hands out to show the squirrel he had no intention of harming it. "Aren't you a cutie? I don't suppose you've seen anyone else around here?" Jasper asked halfheartedly.

As his neck loosened up, Jasper continued to scan his surroundings. The trees all looked the same to him. He could have sworn he saw the exact same tree three times in three different locations as he surveyed the immediate area. Everything looked so similar that he was surprised he did not see another Jasper wandering around in a mirrored direction.

"McMichaels!" Jasper shouted only to once again hear a hissing response from the tree. "Look, I don't need any attitude from you," Jasper said, squinting up at the squirrel. "Unless you have some sort of idea on how to get outta here, I would appreciate some silence."

Jasper began to side step his way down the hill. His feet nervously slid under a thin layer of leaves when suddenly something small struck the top of his head. He looked down and saw an acorn. With almost complete certainty, he turned back towards the squirrel. Sure enough, the squirrel was holding another acorn above its head, ready to drop it.

"Very charming," Jasper said, before giving the squirrel an obscene hand gesture. He continued to wander downhill, grabbing hold of skinnier trunks of the younger trees. The leaves loudly objected to Jasper's weight, but he ignored their complaints and continued to wade through them.

Despite the warnings of the forest, every child in the Village was taught the basics of survival in case they ever, for some inexplicable reason, were trapped beyond the threshold.

The most important lesson was to always wander downhill; down is home. Still the teachers insisted upon expanding into an entire safety session. They would say, the first lesson is to not panic; under no circumstance should a person let the forest know that they are scared. They believed the forest could feed off fear. One person in Jasper's class claimed that his parents once saw a tree sprout out of nowhere when they were collecting herbs, and the more they screamed, the taller it grew.

Jasper used to laugh through all the classes and fall asleep. After all, he and McMichaels had wandered around the outskirts of the forest since they were kids. Now, standing amongst the ominous trees, with almost no sunlight, the harsh reality only sunk in further. Thinking of the forest as a joke became difficult. Every sound he heard, even when he knew it was the shifting and crunching of leaves beneath his feet, tickled his nerves. And every breath he took was another second ticking away before the forest claimed his life.

The occasional scent of scat made Jasper nervous that he was not alone and possibly being hunted. Jasper found confidence in remembering the simple lessons of survival. He reminded himself that each step he took downhill was another step home. He continued to wonder where McMichaels was, but every second he stood still, he heard a ticking clock, counting his life away.

III

Jasper could not tell if he was dizzy or if the forest was shifting beneath his feet. However, he grew nervous and confused when he looked down and saw that he was somehow uphill from his previous step. He had not strayed from the path or stopped walking. The forest had spun around beneath him. In the distance, Jasper saw a shadow shift. "It's just a deer," he muttered to himself as he trudged forward.

A familiar hiss came from above Jasper and he felt something hard bounce off his head. "It's you again, isn't it," Jasper said, slowly looking up. His eyes had fully adjusted to the dim lighting of the forest. The same chubby brown squirrel sat ten feet above the ground.

"What's gotten you so upset? I didn't mean to interrupt your breakfast," Jasper said, feeling calmer. "Can you tell me if you saw anyone else here?" he laughed after he asked.

The squirrel shook its head and climbed down the trunk of the tree. It smelled like roasted almonds and peppermint. Jasper tried to ignore his confusion and asked another question:

"Have you seen my friend?" Jasper sounded more serious this time. He waited in anticipation, wondering if the squirrel actually understood him.

The squirrel shook its head again, this time jumping off the branch and on to Jasper's shoulder.

At first, convinced he was being attacked, Jasper flailed his arms and tried to throw the squirrel off, but it easily kept its grip until Jasper tired himself out and leaned against the base of the tree.

Panting, and almost completely out of breath, Jasper nodded at the squirrel. He looked up at the trees, wishing that the leaves would part a bit so he could see just an extra morsel of sunlight.

"Do you have a name? Probably not. Do you like Bingo? I'm gonna to call you Bingo. Do you know how to get outta here? Of course not, you're just a squirrel. But if you do I'd appreciate it," Jasper continued talking to himself. He deepened his voice when he answered his own questions.

Bingo shrugged and then continued to nibble on his acorn.

"I figured," Jasper said, looking downhill. The trees grew so close together that he could barely see thirty feet away. He grabbed the nearest branch and held on to it as tightly as he could before swinging himself downhill. Once he went as far as the branch would allow him, Jasper released it and let gravity carry him to the next tree. Side stepping around the base of the second tree, Jasper extended his arm and let himself fall downhill again, wrapping his arms around a younger tree's skinnier trunk. He repeated this movement again and again, but soon his body began to ache from checking against dense trunks and sharp bark. He wanted to stop, but the thought that at any moment he might disappear kept him going. "It hasn't been three days," Jasper said, holding on to a branch and hunching over to catch his breath. His tongue felt a little dry in his mouth and he fantasized about pouring a bucket full of water down his throat.

Jasper prepared to reach for the next tree, but something felt off; leaning against the trunk, Jasper scanned his surroundings, but it all looked the same. He was taught that up and down were the two directions the forest could not change, but he was somehow convinced he was going the wrong way. Not even an hour ago the forest seemed to have changed directions mid step.

Jack's stomach rumbled. He tried to comfort it with a deep breath, but that just irritated his dry throat. He could feel his lips cracking. "Please tell me there is a stream around here," Jasper said to Bingo. However, Bingo was chasing his tail and rolling on the ground.

He heard a loud rumble and felt its vibration beneath his feet. Bingo immediately ran back up into the tree. Jasper looked around, desperate to see what caused the sound. The rumble repeated. Bingo cried frantically trying to get Jaspers attention. He waved his paws as if he were drowning. Out of his peripheral, Jasper saw a green blur. He turned and saw the forest floor rising and lowering like a wave under a carpet. It moved toward him fast. The rumbling grew louder and vibrated up Jasper's leg.

Completely paralyzed in fear, Jasper watched the wave rush towards him. Bingo continued to cry out. Jasper felt his legs beginning to give way. A warm fizzing sensation bubbled behind his knees and made standing on his own nearly impossible. Jasper wrapped his arms around the nearest tree as tightly as he could and braced himself.

The wave collided against him. It knocked Jasper back almost ten feet into the trunk of another tree. The grooves in its bark were deep but not sharp.

The jolt of pain recharged Jasper's strength like a bolt of electric fear. He limped towards Bingo, who was still frantically screeching. As Jasper reached Bingo's tree another rumble vibrated beneath his feet.

"Crap," he muttered to himself, looking around to see if anything was charging him. Jasper wrapped his arms around the tree and despite the rough surface grinding and clawing against him; he wormed his way up to the first branch and barely wiggled himself over it.

"Not today. Not yet," Jasper repeated to himself. The farther Jasper got from the ground, the calmer Bingo became. Jasper could hear the tree hum like a tuning fork as the ground vibrated again. This time an even larger wave of grass crashed against its base. Out of the dirt emerged what looked like teeth. They clamped down where Jasper had been moments ago.

Jasper covered his mouth with both hands. His heart beat against his throat so hard he half expected it to shoot out of his body. Another wave struck the tree from the opposite side. There was no mistaking it; teeth marks marred the side of the tree. They scraped against the trunk, leaving deep hollows.

The rumbling began to soften; Bingo eventually crawled to the ground and seemed at ease. He sniffed the surrounding area. Jasper assumed he was searching for food.

He followed Bingo down the tree, assuming Bingo knew it was safe. His legs were still shaking but Bingo's confidence calmed him. "How much time do I got?" Jasper asked Bingo, who ignored him. "Of course," Jasper added, fanning himself off. His shirt, freckled with sweat, pressed against his body. It itched and tickled, but Jasper tried to ignore it. As he began to make his way downhill again, he heard a quiet rush of white noise. Turning in place, Jasper walked towards the sound. The closer he got, the more it sounded like running water.

Before he could break into a run towards the stream, Jasper felt something tugging at his leg. Bingo was grabbing on to his slacks and trying to pull him back on to the path. He yanked with all his might. With puffed cheeks and his eyes closed tight, Bingo almost looked human. Jasper debated listening to Bingo. After all, he was right about the earthquakes moments ago. But as Jasper looked downhill, he could not help but focus on how desperately he needed a drink.

He easily pulled his pant leg away and walked over to where he thought he heard the stream. He was not able to see too far ahead, but the sound of rushing water grew louder.

Bingo stayed back, sniffing around the tree he hid in during the rumbling. Jasper soon lost sight of him. A small spark of fear ignited but his thirst easily extinguished it. The thought of a mouthful of water easily put the fear of death on hold. The sound of running water grew so loud, Jasper thought he might be walking over it, but all he could see were leaves and dirt.

And then Jasper felt something shift under his foot. He nervously looked down, expecting to see the teeth from the earth rising again. But as if standing on a floating sheet of ice, Jasper began to slip downhill. He fell on his back and the leaves beneath him scattered.

There was no stream. The earth was flowing like a river. Jasper attempted to grab on to anything he could find; he rolled around frantically, grasping at dirt and twigs. Looking over his feet, Jasper saw he was heading towards a cliff, which only moments ago did not seem to exist. Nothing stood in his path to stop him. He could not grab hold of anything except soft dirt. He clawed at anything he could but to no avail; brown grains of earth slid through his fingers like grains of dry sand. This was it.

A sudden snag and a sharp pain in his shoulder, but Jasper fought it off and wrapped his fingers around the object that had caught him. Unsure of what he had found, Jasper rolled over and grasped it as tight as he could with both hands. He pulled it to his chest as if he had caught his heart and tried to force it back through his ribs. Thankful his salvation turned out to be a steady rock, and Jasper was able to wiggle his way out of the current.

A sense of nausea quickly came and passed. His throat felt cracked and dry but he could not stop breathing from his mouth. The air itched and forced him to cough every couple of breaths. He peered down stream and saw dirt and mud flowing off the cliff into nothing. Where was it going? It yawned into an infinite void. For all Jasper knew the other side was the other end of the universe and every higher power was sitting cross legged at the entrance. The sight began to make Jasper feel light headed so he backed away from the edge and rested.

Barely able to breathe, Jasper reclined against a rock and tried to stare up through the dense leaf ceiling. He pretended to see the sky so that for a moment he could feel at home. His stomach was telling him that it was almost time for dinner.

The earth rumbled again. Jasper looked both ways, expecting death to greet him on all fronts like an army. He could not decide whether to run or just accept its greeting as a bargain for a quick exit.

Another reverberation sent a shock up Jasper's spine. He felt a warm puddle spread down his inner thigh, as the fear inside him grew too large to contain. The warm dampness pressed against his leg.

As if descending from thin air, Jasper spotted Bingo squealing and running in circles. He reached over to cup the squirrel in his hands as a desperate effort to not spend his final seconds alone. However, Bingo dug his teeth into Jasper's forefinger and ran off.

For a moment Jasper was certain that he saw Bingo wave for him to follow behind. He looked up the hill as the roar sounded more frequently. Over the lip of the hill Jasper could see what looked like a boulder racing toward him like a lost lover. Deciding not to return the affection, Jasper sprinted after Bingo; he followed the nearly transparent footprints left behind on the shifting leaves.

He saw a clearing ahead with what looked like an open path heading down hill. Looking over his shoulder to see if anything had followed him, Jasper was ready to find a safe place to camp for the night. He pulled at his pant leg, hoping it would dry off soon. It stuck to his leg and made walking uncomfortable.

As Jasper began another descent, he felt déjà vu strike the back of his head. Sitting up in the tree was Bingo, with another acorn cocked over his head.

"What do you think you're doing? Trying to keep me here?"

Bingo squeaked a response before throwing a second acorn at Jasper.

"No, not another word from you," Jasper said, taking another step downhill. Bingo's screeches grew louder but Jasper ignored them as he reached for the next trunk. The exhausted muscles in his legs thanked him as he raised one after the other allowing gravity to push him down the path.

IV

Jasper felt as if he had first woken up in the forest a lifetime ago. He was scratching his forearm hard. Flies buzzed around his head and various insects bit his neck and calves. The trees began to thin out and small puddles of sunlight reached the forest floor. However, Jasper was only able to bask in them for a short moment. Sunset loomed--it was only a matter of time. "Two days left," Jasper said. The hair on his neck stood on edge.

Bingo's screeches grew fainter and fainter as the air seemed to spread thinner and clearer. Jasper nervously cracked each of his knuckles as he kicked a pile of yellow and red leaves. It had been a long day and Jasper had still not fully recovered; he held on to trunk after trunk for support as if he were walking through a slalom course, using the trees as permanently placed walking sticks.

Leaning against a tree, trying to slow his breathing, Jasper looked up and through a large opening and saw a small group of stars; he might as well have been lying in the field outside the village's small, stone, wall. "What I would give for a cup of tea right now," Jasper folded his hands behind his head and cracked his back. His favorite spot in the field was a small, loosely kept patch of grass. Jasper used to lie in it, and let the tall blades frame his view of the sky, as the stiff green grass shaved his cheeks and chin. He and McMichaels used to try to count every star in the sky when they were younger. Even as they grew up, they would sometimes count to pass the time while their Colni tea cooled off.

Jasper found a way to keep moving. The trees continued to thin as he descended; it seemed like even the trunks were shrinking, as the dead branches became lively pines.

The same pine trees that Jasper used to stare at from the roof of his home when he was a child. He knew the pine section of the forest was vast; he was encouraged to see that he was moving in the right direction. "Almost home," he said longingly.

Jasper remembered running towards the forest with all the other pseudo courageous children. They used to sneak past the field workers' wood cabins, just outside the farmlands. They would grab whatever they could and charge the forest. Most of the children would throw rocks, challenging the trees from a distance, knowing that the safety of their homes was a short sprint away.

There was a howl from the distance but Jasper ignored it, as well as the shuffling of leaves and cracking of branches that had startled him hours ago.

The beaten path slowly disappeared. Jasper could not say whether the trees were moving closer together or if he was imagining it. As if by some form of asexual reproduction, the trunks of trees seemed to split from another only to form another condescending carbon copy blocking his path home. The pine needles blended into one plane, an indistinctive blur, but the branches, with fuzzed edges, raised a green fist, building the anticipation of a punch.

Jasper was unsure, when he opened his eyes, if he was punched into a coma or waking up from a blink. It felt like he had to swim up through a mile of sand to regain consciousness. The right side of his face felt as if it were slapped by a burning plank of wood. He crawled back until he bumped into what he assumed was the remnants of a dead tree. He heard something moving inside but did not turn. The darkness obscured his vision and he did not want to draw any attention to himself in case something was watching him.

He stared up and saw the only spec of light that comforted him; a lone star stared down on Jasper to let him know that the forest had not yet taken his sight.

Relieved for only a moment, Jasper stared at his stark black surroundings, wondering if his eyes were rolling into the back of his head out of boredom. If only the tree had knocked him unconscious for a few more hours, he would have either woken up to light or never woken up again; both of which sounded appealing. His knees stung from cuts that he could not see. He pulled them to his chest as he attempted to fathom the idea of spending a night in the forest.

Although breathing became easier, his nerves still attempted to suffocate him. A red, misty orb manifested through the darkness. It swirled towards him as if trying to waltz, but stumbled every few steps. A yellow spark snapped from the back of the orb and crackled into Jasper's peripherals; the colors stomped across the now dry earth as if daring the forest to burn.

Jasper reached for the yellow sparks when a blur of green brushed his hand away, blowing a lukewarm breeze up his jacket. The hair on his armpits tingled. The three colors collected in front of Jasper and swirled into a small cyclone, illuminating the void to show the utter emptiness of Jasper's premature graveyard.

Feeling his stomach tighten into a skipping rock, Jasper marched towards the light only to trip face first into a patch of dry leaves. They scratched his face and clung to his skin. He could hear the colors snicker when he peeled the leaves from his cheeks. The lights climbed and scattered; they morphed into different shapes.

Hoping to find a lazy end, Jasper rolled through the darkness; he kept his eyes sealed and listened closely to the whistling of what he imagined to be murderous foliage surrounding him. Every two seconds he hoped to smash into a rock or fall off some cliff, but nothing stopped him.

As if attached to a pulley, the sun rose as Jasper rolled and for the first time since he woke up in the forest, he could feel the dry heat of the sun beating against his face. He could feel the sweat on his skin glisten and tighten. At first he tried to block its rays. He did not dare look in its direction when, suddenly, a thought occurred to him. If the leaves were scattering enough to reveal the sun, he must be getting close to the threshold. Opening his eyes in anticipation, an old optimism returned.

Stumbling to his feet, after tripping the first two

attempts, Jasper looked back expecting to see the colored swirls mocking him. But they had long vanished.

After two steps Jasper felt dizzy and lightheaded. The ground spun beneath him; Jasper held on to a skinny branch and swallowed his nausea. The trees continued to part like the waters of the red sea. He reached out to grab another for support but like a smart fighter, it almost shifted away, allowing Jasper to fall again.

"Dammit!" Jasper shouted through clenched teeth. "McMichaels, where are you?"

As Jasper found his way back to his feet, he looked around the forest, hoping to see any form of human life. Three deer skipped off in the distance. The fawn, trailing behind paused and stared at Jasper for a long moment, before catching up with its family.

"This place was a lot prettier from the outside." Jasper thought about drinking tea on the low, stone wall surrounding the village. He and McMichaels would collect Colni from the border of the forest and brew a small pot over an open flame by the lake.

One of the many reasons Jasper and McMichaels became such good friends growing up was because they both loved the Colni flower's euphoric and soothing effects. They used to steal it from McMichaels' father. However, they started collecting it themselves as his stash dwindled, and when they could not afford to buy it elsewhere. A large patch of Colni grew just along the forest's threshold. They always ran the risk of being caught, but even if they did, McMichaels had a talent for getting out of trouble. After they brewed a cup they would pretend they knew what was out there. Jasper always thought the other end of the forest was a thriving civilization. He knew their ancestors left a distant homeland to start a new life in the village and always wondered what was happening in that part of the world. McMichaels just thought the forest never ended. If it did, surely it only opened onto yet another village.

Some of the elders in the village spent their entire lives studying the forest and the way it interacted with the world. A few could even predict the reactions of the forest's perimeter to certain outside actions. Dobius proved that the forest would shift whenever a living outsider entered; he proved this by throwing rocks, food, and whatever else he could into the forest before wandering in himself. Though the forest did not rearrange for the objects, he claimed it shifted like a maze when he ventured within its depths. Dobius learned that no matter how much the forest shifted, one could always find their way home by walking downhill. He left a trail of various, brightly colored objects to follow home. He noticed that the rounder objects rolled downhill, and realized on a second venture that the village remained downhill no matter how much the forest shifted.

The forest was always Jasper's favorite lesson in school. His old teacher Brytesworth ventured deeper into the forest than anyone else in the village had. Most adults in the village truly believed that the forest had a dark connection to some form of the underworld. But like all supernatural matters, all of the villagers had to come up with their own theories. Brytesworth assured Jasper and the class that these theories were born from ignorance and hysteria.

Brytesworth told stories about her journeys into the forest, and though she mentioned several events that she could not explain, like the pathways mysteriously changing and shifting, she truly believed the forest was just a living body like anyone else; it just happened to be infinitely larger.

"You can't just wander into the forest out of sheer curiosity," she would say. "You have to, at the very least, respect it. Like us it can be flattered, it can be scared, and it can even be angry."

Maps of her adventures dotted the classroom; some were inked on paper while others were built up with small pieces of wood to show the dimensions. Jasper always took the back corner seat closest to the window so he could look out at the forest.

Jasper stopped going to school for a while after Brytesworth disappeared. She was convinced there was more beyond the forest to explore, but none of the villagers believed her; some even began to hate her. The village barely looked for her after her disappearance. The elders sent a couple search parties into the shallow entrance of the forest to plant trails to aid Brytesworth in finding her way home, but she never returned.

That did not stop people like Senior Elder McMichaels from using her memory as a war cry. After her disappearance, a growing majority of people wanted to start attacking the forest. They wanted to clear it, tree by tree, until nothing remained.

A large crack startled Jasper out of his daydream. Desperate to hide from the source, he fell to his knees and crawled into the closest shrub. When he was waist deep into the foliage, he noticed the pink petals of a familiar friend. Though completely exhausted he excitedly looked ahead and noticed more flowers sprouting up. "The Colni!" he exclaimed. Jasper looked through the patch, hopeful to see the threshold. He had only ever seen the Colni close to the entrance to the forest.

Jasper scanned the surrounding area. Once he was

sure the coast was clear, he continued to journey down the path. One step turned into a skip and soon Jasper was running. He leaped off bulging roots and skipped across freshly sprouting grass. Jasper noticed new and younger plants growing as more sunlight fought its way through the thinning leaves and pine needles.

Though his legs burned, Jasper pushed on. His throat and nostrils seared, but Jasper ignored it. A small part of him feared that if he stopped running the forest would change and he would be completely lost again.

However, as Jasper continued down the path, the sight in front of him did not seem to get any closer.

Desperately needing a break, Jasper bent over, holding himself up against a tree, and spit a few times into a bush. He felt something hit the back of his head. Too nervous to look up and acknowledge his worst fear, Jasper closed his eyes and thought about his home.

Another sharp pain bounced against the back of his head. Jasper could hear the same condescending snicker that followed him around since he first woke up in the forest.

He finally turned around and to absolutely no surprise saw the light brown fur of Bingo sitting on a branch ten feet above him.

"Shit," Jasper nervously looked downhill. To some

mild belief Jasper was staring at the same sight he had been chasing for the past ten minutes. The Colni flower still grew at his feet.

"Bingo, is that really you?"

As if understanding the question, the squirrel climbed down the tree and ran up Jasper's arm; it perched on his shoulder.

"You've got to be kidding me. How'd you find me?"

Bingo shrugged and began to nibble his acorn.

Jasper felt awkward standing still in the forest; his fingers and toes were tingling. "It's only been a day," Jasper tried to convince himself again. Something shifted behind him and Jasper jumped. He imagined a snake jumping out of the bush to claim his life for the forest. But Bingo's calmness helped Jasper regain his composure, and he continued downhill.

V

At first annoyed by the sudden wave of sunlight dampening his face and causing him to squint, Jasper soon looked up in excitement. For the first time since he woke up, in what could only be described as a hellish playground, he was able to see the sun, and not just a stray ray or a distant relative. He stood in a pond of light, bathing in the heat, and for an instant Jasper could pretend that he was home.

However, after hopefulness left his mind, Jasper was left with longing and despair. The downhill walk felt more like a spiral through seven circles. However, each time Jasper looked down and saw the familiar pink petals, growing closer and closer together, he felt a soothing tingle roll up his back and down his arms. His stomach grumbled and he was desperate for food and drink. As he walked, growing pools of sweat pressed against his armpits. His dry tongue seemed ready to crack after every breath.

Jasper picked a petal from a Colni flower, rolled it in his hand and sucked on it. His tongue was too dry to taste the flower but he could feel a bit of moistness tickle the back of his throat.

Jasper was limping. His right ankle was stiff and every time he put weight on it, it felt like it might give out. His shins were sore and he had to take a break every twenty feet. Everything seemed to stand still; he felt as if he had been wandering for decades.   Jasper looked around, expecting the earth to grow fangs again and try to swallow him whole. He half hoped it would. Anything to get out of the forest's grasp. He gazed up at the trees, wondering if they were going to swing their branches like fists again and beat him down.

Another vibration crept across the ground. A twig snapped nearby and Jasper fell to his knees. He was far too exhausted to even think about fighting. Bingo, with some new found courage, chose to walk toward the sound instead of running away.

Jasper watched his bushy tail wander uphill towards

the unknown source, but he could not follow. He struggled now just to keep his eyes open. He could smell his body odor spreading and wondered if it would poison the plants surrounding him. There was a high pitched squeak from up the path.

Jasper was not sure what overcame him but he found himself crawling towards the noise. It took every ounce of willpower to pull himself forward, but he dug his fingers deep into the ground and dragged himself toward the cry.

A slim man rolled to his back against the nearest tree. He had a twig stuck in his red curls and a few leaves were glued along the side of his head. Pressing his back against the trunk and sliding up, Jasper made out the pale, gaunt features of the man's face. He had amber eyes and high cheekbones.

"McMichaels?" Jasper asked in astonishment; he expected it was all a trick.

"Who be there?" McMichaels mumbled through chapped lips, still rubbing the back of his neck. His eyes were half closed and Jasper could tell they were adjusting to the dim light.

"Really?"

"Yes? Who-" McMichaels paused. Was it a strong scent or did he recognize something else? McMichaels' face softened and almost broke into a smile. "Jasper? Is that you?"

The two men stood in silence before breaking the mute barrier and pulling each other close for a tight hug.

"What happened? How did we get out here?" McMichaels asked, holding Jasper at arms' length and clasping his shoulders. Jasper did the same, half expecting McMichaels to suddenly disappear.

"I have no idea. I woke up here maybe a day ago. I am not exactly sure how long. But it has been Hell. Last thing I remember was avoiding Judy with you," Jasper said.

"You don't think she put us here, do you?"

"I have no clue how we got here. But I don't think she wanted to kill us. Besides, you're the reason she got to spend time with her idol. Her whole career depends on you making a fool of yourself back home. She couldn't have you disappear forever." Jasper patted McMichaels' shoulder again. He was relieved his hand did not pass straight through.

"My head is killing me. And my mind is so blurry I can barely remember my name."

"I'm just glad you're okay."

"I wouldn't say okay, but I get your point," McMichaels responded, rubbing his temples.

The two turned in a circle evaluating their situation.

The forest seemed to huddle closer and closer to itself as they turned. Intersecting branches and leaves almost completely blocked the sky that Jasper once looked towards as a song of relief.

"So what's the plan now? Die in the most relaxing fashion possible?" McMichaels asked. A few twigs cracked in the distance. It sounded like a snicker, as if the forest found this comment amusing.

Suddenly, Bingo squealed and jumped up the nearest tree.

"Crap! This again?" Jasper said before quickly following Bingo's lead.

"What do you mean by that?" McMichaels asked. Though he did not wait for an answer. They climbed up to the same branch as Bingo and looked down, expecting the worst.

Jasper almost expected a full demonic incarnation to spawn from the forest floor. He imagined the dirt and leaves swirling together in a whirlwind of disaster. "Not yet," he said to himself. He knew it was a shallow attempt to comfort his nerves. He tried to convince himself he had not been in the forest for three days, but his own thoughts seemed to lie.

He looked over to McMichaels, who surprisingly looked calm. Most likely because he had been in a mild

65

coma while Jasper had seen some of the power that the forest actually possessed.

A loud thump crashed in the distance. Seconds later a gust of wind nearly knocked Jasper and McMichaels from their perch. The thump repeated, as did the gust. Thick, warm air clogged Jasper's throat.

The footsteps grew louder. "I'm gonna be sick!" McMichaels grabbed his stomach after another violent vibration shivered the tree. Jasper could feel his grip slipping. He half hoped that he would fall. At least falling to his death would be easier than facing whatever was moving towards him. He even considered jumping.

But the forest would never allow it. If it were merciful it would have either allowed him to die or escape instead of misleading him from one trap to another.

Jasper looked over to McMichaels who, somehow, still looked calm. He snapped his fingers in front of McMichaels' face, but before he could see any reaction, another gust of wind nearly blew everyone off the tree. Even Bingo had trouble holding on.

"McMichaels," Jasper whispered and poked him. No response. The footsteps came quicker, as did the gusts. Soon it was like a drumroll and a hurricane blasting the tree.

Unable to hold on Jasper fell into grey swirls and

white light.

VI

Click.

A green foundation emerged from the blank eternity, followed shortly by a sprinkling of red and orange. As his vision became clearer, Jasper found it easier to breathe. His heart slowed down and his sense of nausea dissipated.

Jasper did not want to move. He only glanced at his surroundings before staring down at his hands. Only a moment ago he could not see them, even if they were inches from his face. Now he never wanted to even blink again. When Jasper finally felt comfortable enough to look away, and sure enough that he would not lose his sight again, he fully took in his location. Though Jasper could move his head, everything below his shoulders felt like it as stuck in mud, and he had difficulty moving around. He could still feel the forest floor against his body. A rock brushed against his foot. However, he could not move.

Not too far away was an arch of light, awash in harsh white and yellow, and Jasper squinted so much that he looked away in fear of losing his sight again. But as his eyes slowly adjusted, he made out the details of the threshold dividing the forest from the village. Jasper turned eager to tell McMichaels, but he was completely alone.

Two arching trees framed the field. The threshold drew nearer, but Jasper remained completely still. The threshold was moving on its own. He stood only feet from the forest exit. However, as he reached for the threshold his nose struck what felt like a concrete wall. He continued in vain to press against the clear barrier and tears blurred his vision.

In the distance, across the field, Jasper saw specs of children running around playing tag. One small boy grabbed his friend by the arm and tried drag him towards the trees. But his friend fell to the ground and curled up into a ball.

A group of girls practiced cartwheels on the walkway next to the pond; and behind them bobbed a boat with two village elders fishing for trophies, only to release moments later.

Without warning, the invisible bind released Jasper's body. He fell to his knees as feeling slowly returned to his limbs. A tingling sensation traveled along his arms and legs. The air was thinner here and Jasper found it easier to breathe. He placed his hand against the invisible divider. To be so close to home but unable to cross the threshold, Jasper could barely take it. Resting his back against the barrier, he folded his arms and bowed his head. He did not want to see his old life. It was a tease and he refused to believe it was real. "You win," he said to the forest. "Just take me already."

Heat from the open sunlight only inches away from his back radiated against the barrier. Jasper realized he was no longer covered in sweat. His thirst had been quenched and his stomach was calm.

He looked over his shoulder again; the field remained the same as before. He was in Hell, looking up through a keyhole at the life he should still be living.

Something snapped. At first Jasper assumed it was in his head but he heard it again. He kept his eyes closed, focusing on where it came from, when something beneath him began to rise. He leapt to the side, pressing against the invisible barrier for support.

When Jasper finally opened his eyes he was looking up at a stone spiral staircase. The bottom steps were wide enough for him to sprawl out upon. But as the staircase ascended, the steps grew narrower. He saw no top; for all Jasper knew it lead directly to the Sun.

Jasper wandered around the base. It looked like concrete but felt like glass. "Is this it?" he asked the sky. "Is my time done?"

Jasper climbed on to the first step. He shuffled around on it for a moment. Once the step felt secure, Jasper jumped up and down a couple of times, pressing his feet against it as hard as he could. Jasper shuffled up to the next step and repeated the process. Each step Jasper took fueled an ever growing sense of curiosity.

Though the wind grew more violent, Jasper never felt any danger of falling. Instead, he felt a warm, static blanket of air shielding him. Each step brought him deeper into its comfort. As he ascended, the light from the sun became a vibrant yellow with streaks of orange; he remembered sitting in the field to watch the sunset behind the forest as a child. He always wondered what lay beyond the trees. In his mind, he always saw an infinitely large garden. Yellow flowers as tall as people and a never ending supply of vegetables. And the people would live in small cabins built on the branches of trees.

Jasper continued his ascent. His first step into a cloud felt like a step into a sauna. The warm thick air blanketed him to the point of suffocation. Jasper lifted his foot for the next step but slipped. He accidentally put all his weight on the edge of the next step and could not keep his footing. But instead of falling to his death, Jasper bounced off an invisible barricade, a force acting as a handrail. At first Jasper was thankful, but as he regained his breath, he felt trapped. Whatever wanted him to climb the steps had gotten its wish. He was now stuck on a single path that even death had to find a detour around.

The air became thin and crisp again as Jasper emerged from the cloud. Though his body still tingled from the warmth below, Jasper could see his breath as he reached a smooth, grey platform at the top of the stairs.

Spiral carvings crawled along its surface. They looked familiar to Jasper, almost like the carvings outside of the garden where the Elders met in the village; almost like the carvings on Elder McMichael's ring.

They intersected with one another. The wind from below came to a complete halt on the platform. Everything seemed to stand still except the clouds beneath him, which sprinted across the sky.

As Jasper walked across the platform, the spirals began to move and shift, circling faster as he drew nearer to the center. Jasper worried he would fall to his death; "Is this some kind of trap?" Jasper asked. He paused for a moment; the carvings continued to swirl. Jasper turned around. The stairs were no longer visible.

He took a few steps back in the direction he believed he came, but there was no sign of any exit. Everything began to look the same. The clouds all shared the same blend of grey, yellow and orange. They rose in imposing walls around the platform. Jasper did not dare touch one. He had a feeling they would crawl through his skin and burn him.

He turned back towards the center of the platform. "Okay, you win. I'm here," he said, shuffling closer to the center. As he drew nearer the carvings, once again, moved faster and faster. When Jasper was halfway there they began to shriek like metal grinding on metal.

Jasper clutched his shirt; his grip was so tight that his knuckles almost turned transparent. The collar bit at his neck. He was only feet from the center when the platform began to shake.

"Here we go," Jasper muttered to himself as he continued to shuffle towards the center. He kept both feet on the ground at all times. The vibrations grew more violent. The platform sounded like it was about to crack. Jasper closed his eyes as tight as he could as he continued to slide his feet along the surface.

His shoulder struck something. Jasper imagined himself in a small, concrete box. It was shrinking by the second. His knees were crushing towards his chin and his arms were pinned to his sides. Even his voice was choked by his receding lips. Swimming back to reality with the urgency of a drowning man, Jasper's eyes shot open. In front of him stood a pale grey figure covered in what looked like tattoos that matched the spiral carvings on the stone. But Jasper could see out of his peripherals that the spirals were gone.

The figure looked like a concrete mannequin. It held its arms folded across its bare chest. Its eyes fixated on Jasper, who found himself unable to hold his gaze, no matter how he tried.

"You have come a long way," the figure said in a quiet yet piercing voice. The sharpness of its tone almost pierced Jasper's chest. His heart beat furiously.

Jasper remained silent. "It's the demon!" he thought.

"Will you grant me the common courtesy of a response?" the figure asked.

Jasper's curiosity slightly nudged his fear to the side for a brief instant.

"My name is Zimriah, I believe it is your turn now."

"J-Jasper," he said through chattering teeth.

"Very fascinating."

Jasper remained silent for a moment. He attempted to swallow the growing lump in his throat. "W-what are you?" He wanted to catch the words but they had already left his lips.

"What am I? I already said I am Zimriah."

"Please forgive me, I am just…" Jasper could not complete his thought. His legs were shaking beyond control now. He knew he was only moments away from death.

"You have nothing to fear, Jasper, I am not going to hurt you," Zimriah said.

Jasper looked up in a mixture of confusion and disbelief. He almost preferred fearing for his life because his mind was too focused on dying to actually be afraid of anything else.

It took a moment for Jasper's eyes to focus but when they finally adjusted he saw Zimriah sitting cross legged with a pot of tea and two cups in front of him.

"Care to join me?" Zimriah asked as he poured the cup closest to Jasper.

Jasper recognized the scent at once.

He sat across from Zimriah and took his cup. The scent flirted with Jasper's nostrils. Zimriah happily drank from his cup and though Jasper remained skeptical, he took a small sip.

"I hope you do not believe that I would poison you over a pot of tea. That action almost defies nature itself. Then again, your people have never been the most harmonious."

"What?" Jasper was not sure if he agreed or was insulted.

"The Colni flower has unique healing capabilities. To poison a living thing through medicine would be treacherous. Especially here."

"Where is here?" Jasper tried to hold his tongue but the more he looked around the more curious he became.

"This is The Garden," Zimriah said taking another sip of tea. The spirals on his shoulder rotated.

"The garden?"

"Yes."

"What's the garden?"

Zimriah put his cup down. "It's where everything grows. I'm sure you're familiar with gardens."

"Yeah, but my gardens have carrots and potatoes, not, well, this," Jasper pointed at their surroundings. The clouds buoyed.

"This is sort of the same. As you choose what

to plant in your garden, this controls the identity of the forest. Perhaps control is not the right word. It protects the forest. If an area is in need of light or dark it will open or close windows for the sun. If a part of the forest is sick it will send help. And if an intruder enters like a virus, it will be eliminated."

"A virus? What have I done? I just woke up here and have been trying to get home before this place kills me."

"You still have time."

"You mean it's real?"

"Of course it's real. Our sole existence depends on keeping you out."

"That's not right at all. That's, that's, that's evil!"

"Evil? Tell me, do you even flinch when someone dismantles my home? Do you eat my food and kill my family?"

"I never have."

"Oh? Very well, have you ever spoken out against those actions?"

"No, but I'd be killed!"

"So it's fair to generalize," Zimriah replied.

"No, there are plenty of people back home who do not approve," Jasper lied, and he had the feeling Zimriah could tell. But Zimriah just took another sip of tea.

"There are plenty of plants and animals in the forest who do not wish any harm upon you, yet you and your kind seem to think everything about the forest is trying to kill you."

"So, you want me to march back home and demand that everyone let go of the fear they've had since birth?"

"No one is born with fear. And I would never ask that of you. Do what you must to survive. And we will do the same. In the end, we already know we will outlive your kind. No matter how hard you may squirm for existence, you rely on a hierarchy. None of you can survive if there is nothing beneath you. That is what will happen. You will fall to the bottom of your chain, and disappear," Zimriah said. He did not sound aggressive or ruthless. He spoke in a matter of fact tone, as if he were teaching basic addition and subtraction in school.

Jasper wavered uneasily in his seat. The stone floor put his rear end to sleep. "So, there is no way I am actually going to make it out of here alive, is there." Jasper dropped his head and lowered his face into one of his hands.

"If all you wish is to return home, you are not too far."

"If all I wish? Of course that's all I want," Jasper said. However, even as he spoke the words he had trouble believing them.

"You doubt yourself?" Zimriah asked.

Jasper did not know what to say. He took another sip of tea. It was like nothing he had ever tasted. The Colni he brewed back home had a small, bitter bite to it. However, this tea almost danced along his taste buds like a thin liquid sugar.

Noticing Jasper's expression, Zimriah added, "This is the proper Colni. The flowers at the forest's edge grow bitter in the sunlight. The true Colni flower grows in the heart of the forest, where no sunlight can reach. Its vibrant pink color blossom enjoys its privacy. It is a rather shy beauty."

"Are you real?"

The carved corners of Zimriah's mouth twitched as he put down his cup. Jasper noticed Zimriah's teeth were the same grey color as the rest of his body and wondered if he actually ate food or just had a mouth to speak.

"Of course." He extended his arm. "Feel for yourself."

"I just," Jasper paused. "I've never seen or even heard of anything like you."

"That doesn't make me any less real."

"Are there more people like you?"

"I am the forest."

"And, beyond your world. Are there other forests and others like you?"

"I do not know. Like you, I have never left my home."

"But what do you mean by that? Is the forest not just your home? I would never say that I am the village."

"I hope that by now you have figured out that you and I are very different."

"What exactly are you then?"

"What are you?"

"I'm afraid I don't follow."

"What would you like to know more about?"

"You speak of the forest like it's human."

"I speak of it like it's alive. Humans are not the only living thing in the world. It is one living body. It feeds itself; it grooms itself." Another long pause. Jasper felt more uncomfortable with every silence. Zimriah was either lying, or proposing such a simple concept that it was embarrassing to not understand. "And it protects itself."

"Yes, but my home does all of that and it's not a living-- not a living..." Jasper waved his hands around, trying to sign a body. "Not a living being."

"Without you, your home would rot."

"And would the forest not rot without you?" Jasper asked.

"Of course it would! And I would rot away without the forest. But if you left your home, you would not rot. No, you would just find a new one." Zimriah walked over to the ledge. The surrounding cloud walls had dissipated. He held his hands behind his back and looked down. Jasper joined him.

He saw the orange light of the sun splashed across the clouds, but he had trouble believing that beautiful sight was the only thing he was supposed to see. He turned towards Zimriah, hoping for sort of clue that would point him in the right direction, but Zimriah stood still. Whenever Zimriah remained still for too long, Jasper thought he looked uncomfortably similar to the statues in the village's garden.

"I can tell there is more you would like to ask," Zimriah said, still staring down through the clouds.

"Is the forest really the spawn of a demon?" Jasper mumbled, half hoping that Zimriah would not hear his question.

"Of course not," Zimriah replied in his usual matter of fact tone. "But plenty of demons have spawned from the forest," he finished.

"What?"

"Why are you only focused on the bad?"

"The bad has been trying to kill me since I got

here."

"That was nothing evil."

"That certainly puts my mind to rest."

"That was just the body protecting itself."

"Still not making me feel too relaxed."

"Your people fear the forest, and with good reason. But there is so much that they should also love." Zimriah turned to Jasper. "It is tough to see past the shadows when you live inside them." Zimriah pulled a Colni flower out of thin air and sniffed it. He handed the flower to Jasper. "But one should not ignore the light in a dark home."

Jasper had collected hundreds of Colni flowers along at the edge of the forest but none like this. Zimriah was right; it was meant to be a vibrant and almost beating color of pink. It warmed his hands like a small sun.

"If you wish to go home, I will grant you a safe journey," Zimriah said.

"Why wouldn't I wish to go home?" Jasper's voice cracked.

"You tell me," Zimriah replied.

Jasper looked back at the flower and smelled it. He could almost taste its sweet scent. "There really is something else out there." He was so sure of this that he did not bother with a question.

"As I said before, I have never left the confines of

these borders." Zimriah turned to Jasper. "But yes. There is a whole world out there, upon which your people turned their backs. Do you know why your ancestors left the world to live in your village?"

"They said the world had killed itself. That man had become too corrupt."

"And their response was to corrupt a world of their own. Two centuries ago, your ancestors settled in a small patch of land surrounding a small pond. The forest's borders used to be much closer. That field was once covered by trees. They left their homes to start a new life. I would be lying if I told you I knew why. Without asking, they cut down our trees, they mutilated our earth, and they abused the land to a breaking point. I felt every cut, every stab, but I could do nothing about it. Nothing, except promise that it would never happen again. So when others decided to follow and find a new home, I made sure they never escaped the forest's borders."

"Oh." Jasper looked over the edge cautiously. He turned back to Zimriah. Zimriah's shoulders were slumped, and his hands were curled into fists. Jasper could not help but actually feel sorry for him. He had never thought about the pain of the land. Seeing the genuine grief on Zimriah's face, Jasper could not help but believe his story. Stone should not be able to flex the way he did. Yet somehow his home had always been able to misshape nature, to do things it could not before.

"Even if that story is true, does that not make the forest evil? It killed those explorers," Jasper asked neutrally. He did not believe his own question. "We were always told that the forest was spawned by dark forces, or was the birth place of a demon."

"It's always easier to kill when it's the right thing to do," Zimriah answered. "Question everything until you find the answers you seek."

"And what if I don't know what I seek?"

"The answers will find their way to you if you look." Zimriah sat down on the edge of the platform and dangled his legs over the side. "Many have died trying to fight their way out of the forest. Many more trying to destroy it. If you wish to go home, draw a circle around yourself with this stick and it will illuminate a safe path." Zimriah reached over his left shoulder and pulled off a spiral carving. It stiffened to a rod after leaving his body. He handed it to Jasper. It was about a foot long, grey and cold to the touch.

Jasper looked up at Zimriah who nodded back before staring up towards the sky. His arms outstretched with his palms up. The spirals on his body began to rotate and slide back into the ground. Zimriah illuminated and dissolving into the light, piece by piece like grains of sand, he disappeared.

VII

Catching himself back into consciousness, Jasper slung his head upright. Bingo clung to his shoulder as the vibrations below on the forest floor grew stronger.

"This is it," MicMichaels whispered as he clung tighter to the tree.

Jasper could feel a stinging warmth flush into his cheeks as he grew angrier by each passing second. "This couldn't be happening. What about Zimriah and the garden of the forest? What about the promise of protection?" he thought.

Jasper clenched his fist in a fit and cocked it back. He was ready to punch the tree when he realized that he was holding on to the metal rod that Zimriah gave him.

Bingo loosened his grip when Jasper pulled the rod out into plain sight. Jasper wondered if it were a coincidence, or did Bingo know what he was holding? Jasper was not sure where the impulse came from but he began to lower himself from the tree. He felt McMichaels swipe at his shoulder in an attempt to stop him.

Jasper's soft stomach scraped against the rough tree as the vibrations came closer to him. Some trees in the near distance began to flip over on to their side, only to be caught by a neighbor and planted upright again.

Jasper leapt to the ground. The fall was a little farther than he thought and a shooting pain jolted up his shin and back. Limping around the leaves, he flung the rod over his head and stabbed the ground with it. The vibrations immediately stopped and were replaced with sounds like crackling firewood. Jasper drew a circle around him and watched the black dirt brighten to a vibrant yellow glow. The light sprinkled out of the ground in a fountain and clung to the ground like wet paint.

A gentle hum came from behind him, and the light continued to jump out of the ground and march towards the sound leaving behind a bright trail. McMichaels remained stiff in the tree. Jasper worried that he was actually stuck in that position and would fall to his death, but moments later McMichaels climbed down from the tree and entered the circle that Jasper drew in the ground.

"What's going on?" McMichaels asked, his voice an octave higher than his usual range.

Bingo ran around the circle. He was squealing in excitement and jumping between Jasper's and McMichaels' legs. Jasper stared at Bingo curiously. He had always found the squirrel odd. Zimriah spoke of the forest as one living body. Jasper wondered if Bingo was in any danger as a native? Perhaps Bingo endangered himself by choosing to travel with him. However, it was not as if he had lured the squirrel into his party. In fact, Bingo sought him out and led him through the forest.

Jasper broke from his thought as McMichaels dug his elbow into his side.

"I asked if you think it's a trap?"

"No, I think it's a peace offering," Jasper replied.

"From what? That vibration? Funny, I don't recall negotiating with anyone. Except maybe a few gods."

"Really? And what did they have to say?"

"I'm not sure. They were quiet the whole time. But when I offered to give up drinking, you jumped from the tree and the vibrations stopped."

"How about that. Good thing you're not a man of your word," Jasper said as he knelt to the ground and touched the glowing earth. It felt no different from before.

"That almost hurt," McMichaels said with a smirk. He was starting to sound like himself again. Living past his expiration date must have given him a second wind of confidence. "So you think this path leads us home?"

"I think so," Jasper picked up some of the glowing dirt. When it left the ground it returned to its natural color.

McMichaels and Bingo began to walk down the glowing trail but Jasper stayed behind. He looked in the opposite direction of the trail, where the vibrations had originated. "What could be out there?" he asked himself, and slowly stood up.

"Are you coming?" McMichaels called. Bingo stood on his hind legs.

Jasper nodded and followed behind Bingo and McMichaels, who began to act careless. McMichaels would jump up and smack a tree branch as if they were playing tag as he skipped along the trail; he also picked a few rocks off the ground and threw them at various trees.

"All downhill from here!" McMichaels said in an even louder tone. Was he trying to draw attention to himself?

After ten minutes of walking Jasper's legs began to burn. Each step became more and more difficult.

McMichaels appeared to be gliding across the ground but Jasper was starting to have trouble even lifting his legs. His muscles begged him to take a break and his fast beating heart matched the cries.

Jasper leaned against a tree for support and McMichaels barely even noticed. Bingo stopped and ran back. His big brown eyes stared at Jasper's legs then up his body to his face with a look of concern.

"How outta shape are ya, Jasp?" McMichaels laughed. "Come on. It's easy. Just lift your leg and let gravity do the work."

"It sure doesn't feel like a downhill walk," Jasper whispered. There was a loud crack, like the splitting of a frozen pond. Jasper frantically looked around to find its source. McMichaels and Bingo continued to walk as if nothing had happened. Another crack sounded, this time even louder. Jasper pushed himself off the tree. Zimriah promised that he would be safe if he stayed on the trail.

"Take cover!" Jasper shouted and leapt to a tree. He could feel McMichaels staring at him.

"What the hell are you doing Jasper?" McMichaels barked. "Quit acting like an idiot. The sooner we get out of here, the better." McMichaels turned his back on Jasper and continued to walk. Some of the pebbles he kicked up rolled down hill and hit Jasper in the face.

"Downhill!" Jasper exclaimed and shot up to his feet. He looked back the way they came and it was now a steep descent. He massaged his burning hamstrings. The path they were following home was taking them up not down.

"Are you coming?" McMichaels shouted again, turning back to face Jasper.

"We're going the wrong way!" Jasper cried. A smile tried to break across his face but it had been so long since he last smiled that it felt like he was dragging his cheeks through wet sand.

"What're you talking about?" McMichaels said, walking back to Jasper. "The trail is leading us home. You said so yourself."

"Yes, but we're going uphill, can't you see!?"

McMichaels looked over his shoulder, back the way he'd come. He squinted for a moment and then turned to Jasper. "Are you alright? How long has it been since you've had water?"

Jasper couldn't quite articulate his next fledgling thought. His mouth opened and closed, again and again. "It isn't home though."

"What do you mean?" McMichaels replied.

"Down is home, but the village isn't down," Jasper wanted to be the voice of reason, but even he could not

91

fully understand what he was saying. He frantically looked around and pulled at his hair, hoping that the answer would come out of thin air.

The two men stared at each other in silence for moment. Jasper was so sure he was right. Everything Zimriah had told him was beginning to click together and make sense.

"Let's just pretend you were right for a moment. Even if the village were up and not down, why would you want to walk back into the forest?"

"Because it isn't home. Think about it. Where do you think we come from?"

"The village. You and I were both born and raised there. We have houses there and our families live there. How is that not home?"

Jasper paused for moment. He was processing everything Zimriah said to him but could not think of any way to make McMichaels trust him.

Jasper told McMichaels about his time with Zimriah as best as he could. He tried to include as many details as he could about everything he learned. Though McMichaels listened patiently, Jasper could tell not much of the information was being absorbed. McMichaels smiled and nodded occasionally but there was no look of wonder or awe on his face.

When Jasper finished recanting the story, McMichaels walked over to the nearest tree and reclined against it. "So you don't want to go back?"

"If I go back now, that's it. I'm going to live on rations, maybe get married and have a kid who will probably starve to death. If I go back now I'm looking at the same walls for the rest of my life."

"So you'd rather die out here? Because that is what will happen. We don't have much time left. Just because nothing bad has happened since we started this walk doesn't mean it will never happen again."

"What Zimriah said-"

"Enough with the Zimriah talk! I was with you the whole time. You sat in that tree with the squirrel and me, hiding. You never spoke to anyone. I thought you died of fright."

"Then how do you explain the trail we're currently following?" Jasper excitedly pulled at the collar of his jacket.

"I can't. Just as I can't explain most other things here. But right now it seems to be the best option for escape. And that's all I want to do."

Jasper paused for a moment. He was not concerned with the fact that Zimriah may have been a figment of his imagination. What concerned him was that McMichaels was right; he did not want to go home. His whole life was built around the village being his one sanctuary, but now he felt like it was just a trap, a place from which he would never escape. The thought of returning to his old job and sitting behind his desk, worshipping the same leaders, terrified him. He looked back at the forest opposite of the trail and longed for answers. "What else could be out there?" he asked himself.

Jasper had not noticed how deep his fingernails were digging into his palm as he continued to wonder what laid past the forest. Even if Zimriah were real and told him the truth, did Jasper even want to know what kind of life extended beyond the forest? According to Zimriah, his people were the ones who chose to leave that place and find a new life.

McMichaels grew increasingly unnerved. Each second Jasper spent debating was like another second stuck in a glass box filling with water.

"Time's up," McMichaels said, finally breaking the silence. "Are you coming or going?" He folded his arms the same way Zimriah had.

"Maybe I was imagining it," Jasper murmured. He tried to push the thought out of his head but it kept creeping back to the front of his mind.

McMichaels turned in place and began to walk

down the trail. He moved slowly, giving Jasper a chance to catch up if he decided to follow. But even with a tortious gait, McMichaels and Bingo eventually disappeared from sight. The trail at Jasper's feet continued to glow, only to illuminate his isolation.

VIII

"Question everything," rang in Jasper's ear. Zimriah
had told him that the more he questioned the more
answers he would find. Jasper turned his back on the trail
and walked deeper into the forest. Though the trail laid
on the same ground, Jasper felt as if he were walking on
jagged cobblestones. Now, back on the raw soil of the
forest he could feel a pulse, some sort of rhythm, beneath
his feet-- a heartbeat pulsing against his soles.

Zimriah said the forest was one living body.
Jasper imagined it sprouting legs and walking away. The
trees grew denser and light went from minimal to almost
nonexistent as Jasper tiptoed through the nonexistent trail.

He turned sideways to slide through a shrinking valley of branches and trunks. The bark brushed so close to his chest that if a tree decided to sneeze, he would be instantly crushed. His jacket snagged on the rough bark every few seconds. Breathing grew harder as he felt himself constrict more and more to the trees' wills. Warm sweater stuck to the side of his body; his lips cracked and his tongue felt constricted and wrapped in plastic. He felt stuck in time, as if stepping into a void. But as the light continued to vanish, through the darkness he saw blotches and shimmers of what seemed like liquid mist, carelessly waltzing through the vacant landscape.

Jasper cut his arm against a tree as the pathway narrowed further. The bark of the trees sharpened here. As he leaned against a tree for support, he felt the trunk of another try to slice open his hand. The ground was so uneven that he had to stop every eight or nine steps to make sure that his feet were still down and his head still up.

The path continued to compress until Jasper felt like he was about to walk into a coffin. His heart raced faster than it ever had before. He was an ant inching towards the heel of a boot, and he consciously made this decision to continue.

"Shit, shit shit," Jasper muttered. He punched a tree and felt the bark cut between his knuckles. "God! Why did I not just go back?" Tears dampened his cheeks. If his front and back were not already compressed against two embracing trees he would've fallen to his knees. Perhaps comfort is the secret to happiness and exploration is the devil's gossip. Was it lunacy to want to see more than the same sunrise and sun set day in and day out?

Jasper tried to remember looking down at the pink and orange clouds when he was in the garden with Zimriah, but each breath he took was a painful reminder that his body was locked in place; his mind could not escape from the constant pressure of the trees and remained as trapped as his body. He had completely stopped moving; through excruciatingly clenched teeth Jasper managed to take a few shallow breaths. He tried pressing his hands against the tree in front of him, hoping to gain even a centimeter of extra space, but his arms had no strength.

Jasper focused hard on his meeting with Zimriah in the garden. Part of him hoped the entire forest would be as tranquil as that place. "You said question everything. How do I get out of here?" he asked the sky. As Jasper remembered the tea that Zimriah gave him in the garden, he unknowingly began to side shuffle through the forest. His body wandered cautiously and his mind did the same. Completely losing himself became easier as the light in the forest went pitch dark. On a stark blank canvas Jasper was able to remember the dark defined lines surrounding the orange clouds in Zimriah's garden. He had practically been standing on a sunset.

The stale, cold air gave Jasper goose bumps up his arm and he could feel the hair on his back brush against bark hooks; he was back in his shifting coffin. His sides had become bruised from brushing against jagged surfaces for so long. Every shuddering breath stung. Despite being outside, the forest passage was too crowded for any fresh air to find Jasper, and he inhaled the same discomfort that had followed him for so long.

Jasper went to take a step but lost his footing. He fell back into a tree. It felt like he was trapped in a small, spinning orb. "Why didn't I just leave?" He sobbed and fell limp against the tree behind him. "There is nothing else out here. What was I thinking? Why can't I just leave? He tilted his head back and muttered a prayer for any kind of help. Every few seconds Jasper would open his eyes and see if light came back to the forest. But no help came.

Too tired to even imagine himself moving again Jasper took off his jacket and slid his arms through it so the back of it covered his chest like a blanket. He folded his arms across his chest to keep the heat trapped against his body. The feeling in his legs was almost completely gone, with the exception of a mild tingle.

When Jasper slid halfway between sleep and reality, he heard something shift in the trees. At first he tried to ignore it, but it snapped him out of his dream state. For a moment Jasper saw a flicker of light between the leaves, but after a second of searching he decided he'd imagined it and closed his eyes again.

After a few long moments of silence Jasper trembled on the cusp of sleep again. But a loud crack snapped him back. It sounded like it was not too far away.

Jasper sprung to his feet and shifted through the trees. He walked with his arms stretched out and used his hands as guides. Jasper desperately clawed through the darkness, hoping to tear it open and reveal the light. Instead he bashed his knuckles against a tree.

Blood ran down his hand. There was another crack, even closer. "It's coming," Jasper whispered. His eyes opened but he could not see through the darkness. Had it been three days? Jasper's heart raced. He grabbed the tree he was leaning against and tried to wrap his arms around it in hopes to climb high enough to avoid what was coming.

Jasper could not get off the ground. The tree was too wide and its trunk was sharp. The bark clawed at Jasper's chest but could not reach his skin; his jacket was still draped in front of him like an apron with sleeves.

Footsteps shifted through the forest. They sounded like they were only a few feet away now. Jasper pressed his back hard against the tree. Daggers of bark stabbed into his skin. His torn shirt was soaked with sweat and blood. He thrust his legs up against the tree in front of him. Pressing into his feet as hard as he could, Jasper began to walk up the trunk of the tree.

He did not get too far. The tree digging against his back opened up a large cut, which caused Jasper to fall back to the ground. He rolled over on to his back and squirmed. The cut stung when it pressed against the dirt.

Too breathless to move, Jasper curled up into a ball. He could feel something hovering over him.

"Rise," a familiar monotone voice said.

"Zimriah?" Jasper asked.

The grey figure appeared with a loud snap; everything else remained pitch black, as dense and dark as space itself.

"Your time is almost up."

Jasper tried to stand up but fell back against the tree. "I can't do this."

"Then be something else," Zimriah replied. Even when he whispered Jasper felt his voice could throw him back.

Jasper could not meet Zimriah's eyes. He stared

down into nothingness wishing the ground would glow again so he could follow it home.

"You brought me here," Jasper said quietly. "I turned my back on my one escape because of you."

"You chose to escape."

"And it's cost me a life."

"Barely. You said it was prison."

"And what's this?"

"Unlike your people, we welcome escape. There is always a safe place to hide, and always somewhere to run."

A clumsy noise came from behind Zimriah. There was no mistaking the sound of dragging feet across the forest floor.

"Jasper? Are you here?" McMichaels cried out.

Zimriah looked down at Jasper and unfolded his arms. He nodded before dissolving into the darkness leaving behind small specs of light, which looked like stars in contrast to the gloom. They floated up, illuminating the forest floor in a gentle white glow.

Jasper turned around to see McMichaels' bruised face. His left cheek was swollen almost completely, closing his deep blue eye shut. The two men immediately embraced.

Bingo scattered across the ground and circled Jasper in excitement. "Welcome back friend." Jasper reached down and pet his chin.

McMichaels gripped Jasper tighter before breaking away. "I was not about to let you have this adventure without me. Lead the way."

"Are you alright though?" Jasper pointed to his cheek. "What happened?"

"Don't worry about it. I was just kind of an idiot who needed to get his bell rung."

"Well you always were that idiot, so I'm glad to hear it finally happened."

"Don't make me regret coming back for you," McMichaels said in a joking tone. He patted Jasper on the back and he followed the opening between trees.

They seemed more spread out than they were before. It was almost as if the forest was encouraging them to continue. "You don't think…?" Jasper was about to articulate the sentiment, but did not want to jinx it. The forest was known to change for intruders, but never to help them.

IX

As the last of the lights that Zimriah left behind faded, Jasper felt a pit in his stomach growing. He doubted it was a trap. But as he failed again and again to find an answer, he grew more uncomfortable. As the last light extinguished, Jasper turned to McMichaels. A look of absolute terror was spreading across his face.

There was a familiar rumble beneath the ground. "Not this again." McMichaels' voice cracked.

Jasper clenched his fists; his nails bit deep into his palms. No matter the ferocity of the attacking monster or demon, he planned on hurting it as badly as he could.

Jasper dug his feet into the ground and crouched

low, waiting. The flat ground shifted and the two men were sent tumbling forward down the previously nonexistent hill. Jasper bashed his arms, sides and head against several tree roots as he rolled. He heard crack after crack, praying that they were from twigs and not bones.

The two men came to a stop; Jasper toppled into McMichaels' back. In an attempt to brush off the pain, they rose to their feet immediately. "Didn't hurt a bit," Jasper lied. He pressed his arm against the closest tree and twisted his back. Every muscle in his body screamed in pain.

A whistle sounded behind them. Jasper turned and took a step forward. As he did, he felt a warm breeze splash his face. A small enclosed area lit up. The soil was light brown, and even blonde in some places. Large flowerbeds full of vibrant, blue, yellow, and pink colors erupted from the earth. Their green roots framed them together. The light seemed to rise over Jasper and create a dome. The rippling light was mostly yellow, but small creeks and veins of different blues and pinks shimmered on its surface. For the first time, Jasper did not see any trees. He looked back to McMichaels but could only darkness. Jasper took another step forward. The earth rippled under his foot. A purple light shimmered across the ground. Staring down at the display Jasper dipped his toe back into the earth. A burst of green shimmered across the ground.

Jasper looked over his shoulder as McMichaels entered the light. His jaw dropped at the sight. There were shadows swimming beneath the dirt. Jasper dipped his toe into another dirt patch. Light swam in circles and a teal wave illuminated the ground. The black outlines looked like fish.

As Jasper explored the rest of the dome, he caught sight of a familiar pink streak. It glowed with the light from the ground and illuminated its vibrant petals.

Feeling a little braver, Jasper took a step out into the fluid dirt and was more than relieved he did not sink to the bottom. He tread carefully across the ground, worried that at any second he could drop into lurking quicksand.

However, before long, he reached the flower. He crouched down to take in its scent and found it even sweeter than he remembered. Jasper reached out and plucked one of the petals. He rolled it in his finger; it was smoother than the ones at the edge of the forest. He slid it across his tongue and sucked on the petal for a moment. He'd never tasted anything so sweet. His tongue danced around, trying to squeeze out every last bit of flavor.

"McMichaels! Come over here now!"

"What's going on?" McMichaels shouted back

stumbling through what looked like a swamp of black lights.

"Here, take this." Jasper rolled another petal between his fingers. He handed it to McMichaels, who immediately recognized what it was and bit down upon it.

The two men sat in silence for a few minutes, nibbling away at the flowers. They dipped their hands into the dirt and tried to move the neon shimmers across the ground into different designs.

"I can't go back," Jasper whispered, finally breaking the silence. He flicked the lingering earth from his hands and turned to McMichaels. In the faint light he could see McMichaels nod.

"I don't think I can either."

"There has to be something more out there. I just really want to know."

"There is!" McMichaels rolled over on his side. "There has to be. It's ludicrous to think we are the only beings left." As McMichaels rolled over, something fell out of his pocket. Despite landing in the soft patch of dirt it clicked and clacked as if it were rolling down a rock face. Before McMichaels could retrieve it, Jasper was able to make out the deep swirling grooves etched across its face. The back came together in a metallic circle. "Is that your father's ring?" Jasper exclaimed, his eyes widening at the sight.

A low groan sounded from the distance. The forest sounded like it was waking up from a deep nap.

"I don't remember him giving this to me," McMichaels said. A gust of wind blasted through their sanctuary.

"Giving it to you? You didn't steal it?" Jasper tried to ask as the wind began to pick up. "You didn't steal it?" he repeated over the gust.

"Why would I steal this?" McMichaels replied, raising his voice. He was beginning to sound muffled.

The ring's design mirrored Zimriah's markings; Jasper was sure he had seen them in the garden. The ground beneath them began to rumble. "Get rid of it!"

"Why?" McMichaels asked. However, as he spoke, the earth vibrated more violently. There was a loud crash just outside of the light barrier.

"Just do it!" Jasper yelled. However, McMichaels could not hear him. Jasper stood up as the wind raged. It almost knocked him off his feet. "Throw it!" Jasper shouted even louder.

McMichaels chucked the ring out of the light barrier. As quickly as it disappeared, the wind died down and the ground steadied.

"What just happened?" McMichaels asked, holding

his arms out for balance.

"I'm not sure. But that ring made this place very angry."

Something brushed through the foliage where McMichaels disposed of the ring. They could hear scratches clawing against the trees and tiny feet scattering across the ground.

Jasper could not find anything through the dark. The light hit an invisible wall and beyond it was pitch black. Jasper shuffled towards the sound. Standing did not advance his line of sight. The noise continued to snap off in different directions.

He crouched low, hoping to hide himself from whatever was out there, but it was no use. He was in the only illuminated area in the immediate vicinity. Whatever it was could easily see him. He took a deep breath before crossing the threshold of light and dark. Immediately consumed by the void, Jasper felt as if a blanket were torn from him in the middle of a blizzard.

Something brushed against his ankle for a moment but it was no use looking down to see what it was. McMichaels looked frozen in the light.

"McMichaels?" Jasper whispered, but to no effect. It was like he turned to stone after staring into the darkness. Jasper attempted to take another step but tripped over a thick root. The tree rattled; Jasper turned and saw a gentle orange glow illuminating its branches. Something about this tree called to him, something beyond his comprehension. All he could see was a small, round orange glow and the branches immediately surrounding it. As he took a step closer, euphoria enticed his body. His limbs tingled as the sensation spread. The closer he moved to the tree, the more it illuminated. Though the rest of the forest was still a black void, the tree was spotted in identical orbs of orange light. The branches crossed one another, making it seem like climbing to the top would be as easy as climbing on a ladder. As Jasper extended his hand to take one, he sensed something moving-- a pulse--almost a heartbeat, coming from the fruit. The rattle from the tree turned into a voice in his head, calling for Jasper to taste its bounty. His stomach turned and tightened in excitement as his hand moved closer to the fruit.

"Jasper!" Michaels cried in a loud whisper.

Jasper turned to McMichaels for only a moment, but when he turned back to the tree, it was gone. He was hit with a wave of disappointment. That fruit had been calling him. "But what was it?" Jasper asked, but he remembered what Zimriah had told him-- "Question everything." He knew the tree was important, but wanted to know why. The sensations that filled his body as he approached it were like nothing he had ever felt before.

A deep hole of dissatisfaction clawed at Jasper's chest when McMichaels called to him again. Jasper walked towards the light barrier and heard something shift in the darkness. Nameless and shapeless, it could be anything. Jasper quickly crouched and blindly scoured the ground for something that might serve as a weapon. As Jasper searched, the shadow revealed itself and began walking towards McMichaels-- it was Bingo. And each step he took made him grow another few inches. Some of his fur retracted into his skin and soon he was three, four, five feet tall. Long legs, and curves soon expanded and revealed themselves along with pale, wrinkled skin.

Bare-naked, standing in front of McMichaels was a woman in what appeared to be her mid-seventies. She had long, silvery grey hair and brown eyes, which were highlighted by the glow of the Colni flowers.

"Ms. Brytesworth?" Jasper asked as he re-entered the circle of light.

The woman turned to Jasper and smiled. Her teeth were flawless. "Nice to see you boys again." She paused for a moment. Looking down at her arms and legs, she seemed surprised at the sight. "Nice to see myself again too."

Jasper removed his jacket and handed it to Brytesworth, who was still admiring herself. The corners of her eyes smiled as she ran her fingers across her stomach. She took Jasper's jacket; it was so large on her that it dropped down to her knees.

"What happened?" McMichaels asked. "Have you been that squirrel this whole time?"

Ms. Brytesworth turned to McMichaels, her smile still sealed across her face. "Whatever you two hit me with, seemed to be something else. I honestly thought it was a rock at first," she said dangling her hands out in front of her face. "What was it?"

"His father's ring," Jasper said pointing to McMichaels.

"What?" Brytesworth asked. There was a flicker of anxiety in her voice.

"What's wrong?" Jasper asked noticing the hesitation.

"That would explain a lot," Brytesworth mumbled to herself. She began wandering around in circles, reaching out at the air as if she were picking apples. "No, can't be, can't be," she said, but her voice wasn't meant for them.

"Can't be what?" Jasper interrupted.

"Nothing," she replied, attempting to sound cheerful. She took a deep breath and flashed her widest smile. "When I was your age, I wanted to desperately be a part of this place. So I ventured deeper than anyone had ever dared to go. That was when I stumbled upon this sanctuary for the first time. It has always been my favorite spot. My sort of secret place."

"What about the ring though?" Jasper asked, feeling a little impatient.

"Whoever brought that ring in here was very foolish," Brytesworth replied. She looked over her shoulder nervously. "Do you still have it?"

"We chucked it over there," Jasper pointed. He was starting to feel the warmth of the light fade away. The way Brytesworth energetically surveyed the area made Jasper wonder if the ring were a bomb or some sort of weapon.

"Okay, good, good, that'll do, that'll do," Brytesworth replied, tapping her fingers nervously together. "I always wanted to be a part of this place." She looked around the barrier

"Why would we be foolish to bring that ring in here?" McMichaels asked. He and Jasper locked eyes, and Jasper knew they were thinking the same thing; Elder McMichaels may have planted the ring on his son.

"That ring, it came from here." Brytesworth said, crouching down and inhaling the closest Colni. Jasper reached over and plucked a petal off. He rolled it into a ball and handed it to Brytesworth, who observed it apathetically for a moment. Then, as if having a sudden revelation, she enthusiastically popped the plant into her mouth and suckled on it. "Yes, it came from here. But it changed."

"What do you mean?" Jasper asked, thinking of the grooves on the ring, the grooves that Zimriah wore.

"Nothing stays the same when it leaves this place. And if something ever returns, the forest recognizes the scent and finds it easier to deal with."

"Deal with?"

"Exterminate, eliminate, kill, destroy, crush, dispose of," Brytesworth continued listing off every word Jasper dreaded hearing. "It's almost like your body dealing with a pestilence it has beaten once before. The forest must've sensed it and been on rather high alert for intruders."

"So the forest made a ring?" McMichaels asked, still clearly disturbed by Brytesworth's rhetoric.

"Oh no, of course not. It was passed down to your father. Someone turned a trophy they found generations ago into jewelry for the highest elder. I'm not sure why, of course, but they pass it down to one another for fun I suppose. My dear, things certainly are making more sense now. I mean I had ventured into this place hundreds of times before changing. But this place really wanted to kill you."

This did not reassure Jasper very much. And

the sunken look on McMichaels' face reflected similar sentiments. They remained still and silent.

"But yes, yes, I can see now. Ha, well, it's gone now. We are safe. For now, I suppose. At least, I think. You don't still have it, right?"

"What? No, you said we hit you with it. It's over there somewhere." Jasper pointed.

"Good, good. Wow, this place is beautiful," Brytesworth said, as casually as if they were just discussing the weather.

Jasper attempted to listen to every syllable meticulously. He was still in complete shock over the sudden appearance of their old teacher.

"My last venture here was different from the rest. Standing in the middle, where you are now, was a large, almost stone-like figure. He was stroking the Colni flowers as if they were his pets. At first I was terrified of this thing. I wondered if all the stories were true and perhaps this was the demon all the villagers feared. But then I thought how could something that is pure evil care for something else? I could understand a Demon having an army, or disciples, but flowers?" Brytesworth continued to rub her arms, as if she were worried they would disappear again. "But before I could act to either engage or flee, the figure turned to me. At first it smiled, but something felt-- off. I was not sure if it was being courteous or genuinely happy to see me. It then sat down cross legged, and as it did, spirals slithered up his arm and across his body like snakes."

"Was he named Zimriah?" Jasper interrupted.

"Have you met it?"

"He brought me to the garden."

"The garden?" Ms. Brytesworth asked. Her face was so contorted that Jasper was unsure if he accidentally offended her or completely confused her.

"At least, that's what he called it." Jasper felt stupid as he trailed off. He must've sounded like a lunatic.

"You mean, you've seen it?" Ms. Brytesworth asked, her voice cracking like that of a twelve year old boy.

McMichaels looked back and forth between Jasper and Ms. Brytesworth. Jasper could tell he looked confused but was more focused on figuring out what Ms. Brytesworth knew.

"You've heard of it?" Jasper asked.

"I've seen it. Not like you. I was led to a flight of spiraling, stone, steps, which appeared out of nowhere. I was, for a little while during my journey, doubting my beliefs and longed to return home. A voice called to me and I followed it, unsure of where else to go. As I approached the edge of the forest I thought the voice was leading me home, but it was as if there were an invisible wall preventing me from crossing the threshold. I assumed it was some evil joke played by the forest, but then I saw the steps rise and rise, until they were above the clouds. The same calm voice called me over to them, but after I was four or five steps up they flattened into a slide and I slipped back down to the forest floor."

"How did you know it was the garden?" Jasper asked.

"Zimriah told me he watched me climb, but could not let me come to the top-"

"But that's not fair!" Jasper interrupted. "No one would've appreciated it more than you. It would've been your paradise."

Ms. Brytesworth raised her hand to Jasper, gesturing him to be quiet for a moment, and smiled. "It's alright. I thought so too, at first, but everything Zimriah does is for the good of this place."

"Same with you. It's all you talked about. You love the forest more than any other villager," Jasper said with so much force that he was out of breath by the end of the sentence.

"Jasper, that is not entirely true."

"What do you mean?" McMichaels asked. His voice cracked, but differently than Ms. Brytesworth's did. He had been silent for so long his mouth seemed to have forgotten proper speaking technique.

"It is true, I was always fascinated by the forest. But it was always for more of a selfish reason than I would like to admit."

"Selfish? You've saved it from angry mobs," Jasper replied.

"Also true, but in some ways I was no better than the mobs. If it were not for Zimriah stopping me I would've destroyed a small part of this forest just for an even smaller piece of knowledge. I was obsessed with knowing as much as I could about this paradise. I didn't care what homes I destroyed, what animals I hurt-- all I cared about was knowledge. That was when I stumbled across this lovely patch of Colni. I had never seen anything like it before. I immediately pulled out my pocketknife and bent over to start collecting samples when I heard a whisper come from beyond the light boundary. There was a gentle glow coming from that small tree you walked into earlier."

Jasper turned his head. Though he could not see past the wall where the light stopped, it felt impossible to forget where the tree was; when Jasper closed his eyes he could still feel a faint heart beat from the fruit, beckoning for his return. He could almost hear his name in its percussion.

"What is that?" Jasper whispered. He looked to McMichaels, who seemed frustrated. McMichaels sat down cross legged and began to stroke the Colni leaves. He clumsily plucked a couple petals, rolled them up in his hand and sucked on them as Jasper and Brytesworth continued to converse.

"I'm, well, I am quite curious to hear what you think it is," Brytesworth said staring back at Jasper. Her fair skin reflecting the glow from the plants like the moon reflecting the sun. A small smile flickered across her face as she watched him contemplate.

"It felt... alive. I know that sounds crazy, because all plants are living things, but this one is different. I could feel a heartbeat. It was almost calling for me."

"Go on, go on."

Jasper paused for a moment as he thought about his encounter. It was difficult to put into words. When he opened his mouth to articulate how he felt, nothing came out. He was flirting with unchartered territory. "It felt like everything good that could possibly happen to me would happen if I reached out and grabbed the fruit. I don't know what to say. It was like defeating superstition; there was something telling me that if I did this one small thing, then righteousness would ripple from the tree and expand across the entire planet."

Brytesworth nodded. "Yes, why yes, yes, I know the feeling. And it was so warm. Not to the touch, it did not seem like it would burn, definitely not, but it was something else that made my body flush with excitement. Oh, so much excitement. A-and when I thought about even shifting my weight away from the tree I could feel a cooler reality slithering through my veins."

"Yes, I know what you mean. It just seemed so powerful. And I didn't understand how. It was just a small piece of fruit."

"What fruit?" McMichaels voice cracked when he asked. "What're you talking about?"

Brytesworth turned to McMichaels. "I am talking about the heart of the forest. I consumed a piece of it once. Just once."

"You what?" McMichaels asked. He turned to Jasper with a pleading look.

"I desecrated the forest."

"And then-" McMichaels began to speak.

"Then I was punished," Brytesworth interrupted him.

"And that turned you into a squirrel?"

"No, no, it did not. Well no, not exactly. No," Brytesworth looked up at the dome of light surrounding them. "At first all the feeling that my senses promised me were over flowing, over saturating, just beyond full. And my body surged with a sense of euphoria. Yes, it was delightful. I can't exactly say how or why, but I truly believed I had accomplished my life's work as soon as the fruit's skin touched my lips. It was just so sweet. But just as quickly as this revelation came, it left, and soon I was standing in complete darkness. I was shivering and felt soaking wet, and oh, so alone. My skin was cracking. The darkness spread beyond my line of sight but I felt so contained that for all I knew I was trapped in a small box on a never ending path. I am not sure how much time passed, but a small speck of light cracked the ground and spread until it was large enough for a large, muscular body to ascend through. At first I could not recognize who or what was floating closer towards me. I feared it was the demon we had been taught was born here, coming to eat my soul. But then I saw a carving slither up his arm and to his chest forming spiral after spiral. It was the same creature I had seen earlier in this field. It was Zimriah. And he protected me from a sentencing I still do not fully understand. If it were not for him, I would had been left there to rot-- or worse."

"How could it be worse than that?" McMichaels asked.

"I'm not sure, but that is one question that never

needs an answer."

"Why did Zimriah let you out?" Jasper asked.

"I am actually still unsure-- he empathized with my curiosity, I think. He could tell that even though I was more interested research than the safety of his home, I would never do anything to permanently destroy this place. To be honest, I was not sure if that was entirely true, but after he said it, it became the absolute truth. He explained that I would have to help repair the damage and live in the forest but did not say how long. I assumed it was going to be like a life of labor, but I was wrong."

"That's when you were transformed," Jasper said.

"Yes. I was transformed and had to live in the forest, at first on my own. I was terrified and thought this was just another form of humiliating execution. But days became weeks and months, and the only interactions I had were other inhabitants trying to help me. And I noticed that as we helped each other and co-existed, strange things happened. A trail of broken roots and trampled plants left by my clumsy explorations would heal and flourish; branches used for firewood would grow back quickly; and the heartbeat from the center of the forest grew stronger. Not to the point where it was before I damaged it. There was once a time when you could feel its vibrations from every corner of the forest. But it grew stronger nonetheless."

"You mean you've been to the edge?" Jasper perked up.

"Of course I have. And it was like nothing I would have expected. Buildings I never imagined and a civilization vaster than the forest itself. In fact, the people there did not seem to even pay this place any attention. It was like the forest did not exist to them. There were a few people who crossed into our borders, but they never wandered too far."

"Can you lead us there?" Jasper said. He walked towards the boundary of the Colni's light as if he already knew the trail.

Brytesworth followed Jasper to the edge and rested her hand on his shoulder. "Are you sure that's what you want? You still have time return to the village, but once you walk out the other side there is no turning back."

McMichaels shifted uneasily in his seat. Jasper noticed and shot him a sympathetic look. "Do you not want to go?"

McMichaels looked down at the ground and dipped his finger into the fluid earth. He swirls a stream of pink light. After a couple deep breaths, he said, "I don't want to get in the way of your adventure, Jasper. Or your life. However, no turning back? Does that not make you feel the least bit worried? We don't even know what else is out there."

"But we know how little is back there." Jasper pointed back the way they came.

"But it's safe," McMichaels paused. "It's home."

"Safe? Did you feel safe at the bar the other night? What about that ring in your pocket? For all we know, your father left us out here to die."

"But we don't know that."

Jasper took a few steps towards McMichaels. "That place is not a life, it's a prison sentence. We are trapped by some imaginary fear and we're free to live the exact same lives as the generation before us until the food runs out."

"But we would be leaving our friends and our families."

"Friends and families? I never knew my family. And friends? The ones who tried to kill us at the bar the other night? Or do you mean your father-- a man who openly demonstrates how little you mean to him on a daily basis?"McMichaels remained silent. Jasper continued his onslaught. "We would be skating through routine conversations and rituals. We live a life where people only pretend to not know every detail about everyone else. Everything about that place is completely choreographed and the end of the performance is hastily charging. And it's not coming from the forest, or mysticism that our brilliant minds are still working on capturing, it's coming from that trap we call home!"

"That trap of a home has kept us safe all these years. It's not like you're some field worker being starved on a daily basis. We were targeted for defending the forest and I have to say, as beautiful as this place is," McMichaels gestured to their surroundings, "I am not exactly over how many times it's tried to kill us."

"We go back we die a slow death, or have kids and let them die it for us,"

"And if we go on, we might not even make it to the edge. Last I checked we have one day left before this place sucks the life from us."

"Not exactly," Brytesworth interjected. "That old rumor is true, I have discovered through my time here. But I have also learned that this place--this heart of the forest" --she waved her hand at the light dome surrounding them-- "is under protection. And anyone within its depths is safe. Think of it like a reset button. No one would be able to make it through the forest in just three days. But this place almost renews your time."

"So what? It's like we have three more days?" Jasper asked.

"More or less," Brytesworth replied. "That was the impression I gathered from my conversation with Zimriah. He wanted you to find this place."

"You've been speaking to him this whole time?" Jasper asked.

"Of course not. Only for a brief moment when we were trapped in that tree. He told me to lead you here for safety and to find yourself. But then you leapt from the tree and illuminated a path back to the village," Brytesworth said.

"Then why did you let us walk down that path?" Jasper replied.

"I couldn't force you to do anything. It had to be your decision."

"Well, if you were supposed to lead us here, why did you keep following me?" McMichaels asked.

Brytesworth smiled. "Because I knew you would need help finding your way back."

There was a long, uncomfortable pause. Even the light within the boundary flickered. Brytesworth seemed to almost glide over to McMichaels, who had dropped his head to his chest and buried his hands in his pockets. She stroked the back of his head. Each finger seemed to linger a little longer than the last.

"I understand the loss of self, better than anyone

else. I have been trapped in this forest in a small and foreign body for decades, and it was not comfortable. I spent my first three months trying to starve myself, but the forest would not let me. I would sleep only drinking a couple drops of tears and wake up full."

"What happened?" McMichaels asked.

"I was not sure at first. It did not make sense to me at all. I should have died dozens of times but the forest seemed to be acting as my guardian. Even when I discovered this I was confused, because why protect me? The trespasser who almost destroyed it? I spent another few months contemplating this strange phenomenon. But all my hypotheses were dead ends. One day, after wandering deeper into the forest than I had ever gone, I had the strangest compulsion to go home; what made it so strange was I was not referring to my vacant bed next to the school back in the village, but a small nest I made in the knot of a tree. It all came together; I had not lost myself but found a new part. The forest had become my home, and kept me safe because I had become a part of it. Do you understand?"

"I think so," McMichaels said unconvincingly, but maintained eye contact with Brytesworth.

"I understand the comfort of knowing who you are. And finding out you are something else is terrifying.

But after a metamorphosis-- once you really discover your body-- you become who you were always meant to be. I cannot force you to do anything. It is your life and your decision. However, what I can say is that you will never have as great an opportunity as you do now to evolve into the being you were meant to be. The fields will die and the lake will dry; the village will one day be forced into extinction or exodus, but either way, you are trapped. Today, you have the opportunity to choose your path and by returning to your friend" --Brytesworth nodded toward Jasper-- "it appears that you have already decided what you want to do. Even if you're trying to battle that decision now, it was still your choice."

McMichaels looked back at the path. Jasper attempted to stare with him but his attention kept being pushed by the palm of a warm hand towards the heart of the forest--the tree. He could hear its heartbeat echoing in his ears, tempting him to sneak into the darkness and consume it. It whispered secrets to him, just quiet enough that he could not make out any of the words. He could see himself holding the world in his palms and drinking the secrets of the universe from its core like cider.

"You're right," McMichaels said, breaking the silence. Jasper wondered if they could hear his thoughts. He caught Brytesworth's eye; she gave him a stern look, a warning to end his dangerous thoughts, and Jasper felt the hair on his arms and neck rise.

"Wonderful," Brytesworh said, keeping one eye on Jasper. She led McMichaels towards the opposite end of the dome and bumped Jasper, forcing his gaze away from the black vacancy, where he assumed the tree still stood. "We are about to enter the darkness again, but it will not linger long. Not many trespassers reach this end of the forest so it remains rather dormant. Give it no reason to pay you any attention and it will stay quiet." Brytesworth left the boundary's light first but kept her hand through the wall of light for Jasper and McMichaels to grab. McMichaels walked through first with his new found energy and excitement. Jasper lingered; he stared over his shoulder, back toward the tree. Though he could not see it, he could feel it tapping against the soles of his feet. He could easily close his eyes and follow the rhythm to the trunk. Debating which direction to offer his next step, Jasper glanced back towards the tree. Brytesworth reached through the barrier and gestured for Jasper to take her hand. After a long moment, Jasper clasped Brytesworth's hand and let her pull him through the light.

For a moment he was completely disoriented and felt as if he were walking toward the sky. Jasper tried pulling his arm away from Brytesworth and walked right

129

into a tree. His nose felt halfway between squished and swollen. His eyes watered from the impact.

Brytesworth yanked on Jasper's arm and whispered. "You are not to let go of me. Either of you. Until we reach light. Do you understand?" Jasper and McMichaels both nodded but Brytesworth only heard silence. "Do you both understand?"

"Yes," they both replied.

Though pitch black, Brytesworth led the two men through the forest without any trouble. Jasper wondered how many times she had wandered this far. If it was indeed a part of the forest that remained in some form of hibernation, it would not change its terrain very often.

Jasper bumped his shoulder against something hard. He took a couple steps away and brushed against what he assumed was another tree. He could feel the roots at his feet meeting closer and closer together and imagined the trees surrounding him almost hugging. Jasper's breath shortened and became shallower and shallower as imagined himself in an ever shrinking box. He could feel the trees growing closer together, and could almost hear them moving closer to him, limiting his movement until he was stuck in a living coffin.

"Jasper, are you okay?" McMichaels whispered. Jasper responded with a few quick breaths. He dug his fingernails into the arm that Brytesworth was holding to distract himself.

"It's closing in," he muttered and started to dig his heels into the ground.

Brytesworth yanked on Jasper's arm and he fell to his back. The roots on the forest floor scraped his back as he was dragged. The top of his head knocked against a couple elevated roots. Jasper quickly scrambled to his feet.

"What do you think you're doing?" he almost hissed.

"Leading you to the edge," Brytesworth responded in a matter of fact tone. "You were not moving so I moved you."

"You could've given a warning."

"That wouldn't have helped. Besides, you seem less scared now. So shut up and keep moving," Brytesworth whispered and continued to lead the way.

After a few hours of complete darkness, Brytesworth stopped. "Look up."

Jasper noticed a small spec of yellow. It was different from the images he had seen in the darkness; those had been blurred blotches of floating color swimming through the gloom like an ocean. The yellow spec had sharp, defined edges and remained perfectly still.

"That's our first real light," Brytesworth said in a

more excited tone.

Jasper could not help but smile and he heard McMichaels sigh in relief.

An hour later, the small specs of light filled the sky like stars. Jasper assumed it must be close to noon and wondered how long they were going to hike. He could still feel a quiet thump under his feet, but every time he hesitated, Brytesworth yanked him back into place.

Jasper's legs screamed at him and he wondered if Brytesworth and McMichaels felt the same. He licked his lips but his tongue stuck to the chapped cracks. His feet began to feel numb and his shins shot with sharp pain after every few steps.

The path seemed to widen and Jasper's breath deepened. He was able to start making out small details around him. The edge of a trunk and the blurred outline of something on the ground.

"We don't have much farther," Brytesworth said. She did not sound out of breath. In fact she sounded as if she would be able to sprint the rest of the way.

"Until the edge?" McMichaels asked, half excited and half breathless.

Jasper felt a small sense of relief that he was not the only one struggling with the journey. He had been too scared to worry about complete exhaustion before and wave after wave of fatigue splashed against him with each dragging step he took.

"Nonsense," Brytesworth responded. "We won't make it to the edge until tomorrow. But we should be able to see the sky very soon. From there it's just an easy downhill hike." Brytesworth tugged sharply on Jasper's arm. He did not realize that he had stopped moving. "Are you alright?" she asked.

"Fine, just thought something moved under my foot," Jasper replied.

"Be careful," she said, leading them a little more carefully through the tight path. "This side of the forest has almost never seen a trespasser before. We are making our own path right now."

"Almost never?" Jasper asked.

"Yes, almost."

"Do you mean besides you?"

"No, I never made it this far," Brytesworth answered. "As a trespasser, that is."

"So-"

"The forest is my home now," Brytesworth interrupted Jasper's comment. "I never made it this far until I welcomed the forest as a part of my identity. The trespassers I speak of were more than a handful of generations ago. Story goes that they were scientists exploring the rumors of a new life form in the forest."

"What, like the story about the demon?" McMichaels asked.

"This was during the very first years of what we know as the village. Back then, there was no animosity between our neighbors. In fact the original settlers and the forest co-existed almost seamlessly. The three scientists journeyed deep into the heart of the forest out of curiosity. Story goes that back then, a person could almost feel a heartbeat if they stood at the threshold dividing the forest from the village. So they followed the sound and it led them to a tree. It was not too far from the light dome where we met. And the men were all drawn there-- it had a loud silence to it. And, supposedly, they all had a hunch it was the life force the forest drew its energy from. It is said that the three men followed a different path to the tree."

"Why would they do that?" McMichaels interrupted again.

"You've seen how dark it is. They were just following whatever senses they could. As they approached, they allegedly heard what sounded like an irregularity in the beat. What they actually heard were footsteps. According to the story, they saw a muscular being, carved from stone, marching towards them. As the three men attempted to escape, the unfamiliar being trapped them one by one and cast them into a chasm he carved out of thin air."

"A chasm out of thin air? Like what happened to you?" Jasper asked.

"Very spooky, if I do say so myself. The first two were cast away immediately, but the third man, who was furthest from the tree dove into the field of Colni flowers. When he opened his eyes the stone creature was gone. Assuming the Colni warded off the evil, the man stuffed his pockets with as many flowers as he could and eventually found his way home. He recounted his story to all the villagers and told them that the forest is the home to a vicious demon. He pulled flowers from his pockets and explained how their presence warded the demon off and saved his life."

"So they--"

"They planted the flowers and their seeds along the edge of the forest for protection and the only survivor from the expedition was treated like a king. See, before then, everyone in the village listened to everyone else like an equal. But this man, he..." Brytesworth paused. "He changed that. What he said became law. They built a statue in his honor. And in order to keep his power, he created the council. An ultimate ranking for officials to achieve by passing what appears to be rigorous tests of intellect, when in reality it is just guaranteeing they all believe the same truth."

Jasper tried to take in everything Brytesworth had said, but as she recounted the story, a gentle breeze whispered across his face and kissed his hair. He looked up and for the first time in days saw the moon.

"This looks like a good place to camp tonight," Brytesworth said, leading the two men over to small patch of earth without any roots lifting the ground. The trees were more spread out than Jasper had seen since being in the forest. He could actually stretch out his arms and legs without touching more than one trunk. The branches were thick, but barely crossed over one another, making the view of the sky almost uninhibited.

Jasper could start to make out the edges of two shadow figures. He could see a blurred and undefined line of what he assumed was an arm patting the ground.

"So that story, well, it's true?" McMichaels asked nervously.

"It was told to me as the absolute truth, so naturally I am not sure if I believe it," Brytesworth replied.

"Why was it never told to us?" Jasper asked as he found himself a comfortable place to sit. He nervously relaxed his back against a tree and was relieved it was not as sharp as some of its relatives deeper in the forest. "Was it a secret or something?"

"I am honestly not sure why we had to keep that story hidden. Your father was the one who told me," Brytesworth said to McMichaels.

"Why?" he asked, perking his head up.

"It was before an expedition. I wanted to see if I could find an exit less than three days away. I am not sure if he was trying to scare me but all it did was fuel my curiosity."

"Maybe that was the plan," Jasper chimed in.

"Why would my father want that?"

"I don't know. Maybe he was too scared to look for himself." Jasper replied, resting his head on his shoulder. His eyelids heavy, and the stiff muscles in his back and shoulders began to relax.

X

As Jasper felt himself sink deeper into sleep, a small thump against the back of his head startled him back to consciousness. He brushed it off at first and nuzzled back against the tree. However, as he curled his knees up to his chest he heard it again. Jasper opened his eyes but it was too dark to see. The thump sounded off; this time it vibrated up his entire body. Before long Jasper recognized the percussion that had lured him from safety before. It was calling him again, beckoning him to follow the beat's path and let the rhythm guide him back.

But Brytesworth had warned him; she had suffered the consequences before. Still the call echoed off the trees, gently flirting with him. It needed Jasper's attention. The forest had always been calling to him. It wanted him to explore. That is why he was welcomed into the garden, where Brytesworth was not. This experience would be much the same. Jasper was chosen. He had to follow the call.

Jasper felt himself gliding across the ground; the uneven roots and cramped path passed by as if he were a ghost. He could have just as easily been floating on a hammock through an open field. It became easier to breathe.

The forest, which he longed to be nothing but a blurred memory when he first arrived, passed by faster than a sneeze. He fell to the ground, out of breath; whatever happened was over. He felt every rock, root, and plant punch against him as he rolled to his stomach. The cool dirt iced his face, which he was sure was cut and bruised.

"What was that?" Jasper asked himself and attempted to lift his head off the ground. He tried to look around, but his back screamed at him to lie still. He lifted his gaze as high as he could before looking into the top of his eyelids. There was no opening to the sky; the roof of branches and leaves were stark black and glaring down in ominous silence.

"Shit." Jasper grit his teeth. Digging his fist into the ground, he tried to crawl back to his feet. The bullying pain pushed him down and kept its foot firmly on his back.

Unable to move, and too tired to be afraid, Jasper closed his eyes and tried to focus on the cool forest floor. He welcomed the icy sensation along his body and focused on its slithering gait as it wrapped its grip around him and soothed his cuts and bruises.

He could feel himself lolling back to sleep. Tomorrow he would find Brytesworth again. Tomorrow the new world would begin. Tomorrow. The orchestra of silence loomed over him and slowly decrescendoed to a single string instrument plucking Jasper along to sleep. His back quieted down from its tantrum and soon he found himself in a deep state of relaxation.

But as he was on the cusp of sleep, Jasper heard a single beat in the ground. It was faint but it sounded like it directly called to him. Jasper felt the pain slowly stalk its way back to him as he focused on the second beat.

He silenced his screaming muscles as he willed his way to his feet; he could feel the heart of the forest calling. His strides lengthened and hastened as he ran deeper, toward the sound. The cramped spaces, which paralyzed his body in fear the previous day, had no effect on him.

The heartbeat quickened as Jasper ran nearer. He

closed his eyes and lowered his head as the branches of the trees cut and slapped his face. The ground vibrated and Jasper felt rocks emerging from the earth trying to obstruct his path.

He could feel a warm glow brushing against his face and passed through the light like a waterfall. A strong gust of wind past over his body. It felt like he had broken his way out of a bag. He looked down and saw the Colni flowers blooming. Only this time they did not release bright, neon swirls when Jasper splashed around in the dirt. They released a harsher, vibrant light, which bounced around the barrier in sharp angular lines. The light passed by Jasper and it felt like the ghost of a sword; it gave Jasper a sharp bite but left no mark on his body. Just a buzz that numbed the skin. He jumped when he saw another line of light gliding towards him.

Jasper struggled to focus on the heartbeat as he rolled and skipped over beams. He ran to the edge of the barrier and focused on the faint sound beating against his feet. It danced up his shins and shimmered along his spine. Digging his bare feet into the ground, Jasper could feel its pulse directly in front of him.

Jasper opened his eyes and saw the ground rippling with white-yellow light. A couple bands of light passed through Jasper's shins and he faltered to his knees before quickly jumping over the next wave. If he could just reach the heart, he could end the fight. All the mysteries of the forest would be revealed to him.

All he had to do was find the tree. Jasper focused hard on the pulse and jumped over another beam of white light. He ran through the flower patch jumping over the attacks as they grew more frequent, a drumroll of strobing energy. As Jasper reached the opposite side of the barrier, something caught his foot and tripped him. He was only down for a second when a spear of yellow ran through his entire body. It felt like lightning. Another passed, and another; he could feel his spine freeze and thaw instantaneously as band after band of light passed through. It felt as if every bone in his body would shatter if he tried to put any force greater than gravity on it. And after another strike even gravity felt like a boulder on an hourglass. Jasper could feel another blast beginning to pass through his body when the violence suddenly ceased. He could feel the light sink into the ground. The loud, buzzing vibration that had filled the barrier during the attack died down.

Jasper finally felt the strength to roll back over to his feet. He had no idea what could have stopped the attack.

He was not expecting to see Brytesworth and

McMichaels standing opposite him.

"What do you think you're doing?" Brytesworth asked. At that moment, her gaze was the only thing sharper than her voice.

"I don't remember," Jasper half lied in response. He did not know why he woke up so far away from camp but after he felt the forest's pulse calling to him, nothing else mattered.

Brytesworth signaled for McMichaels to stay where he was as she almost glided towards Jasper. Jasper nervously rubbed his arms and the back of his neck as Brytesworth drew nearer. She had a look of determination in her eyes that Jasper had never seen before. He worried for a moment he would melt from exposure if he stared too long.

"You were returning. Yes, I see that. Returning," Brytesworth mumbled. Even in a whisper Jasper felt her words knock the wind out of him.

Jasper remained silent. In one ear was the roaring drum roll of inexplicable euphoria and in the other was a silent wrath he wished to never discover.

"You must fight that urge. I was a prisoner. Far worse could happen to you if you make the same mistakes I made. Not only would you be betraying its hospitality, you would be ignoring a clear and honest warning. Clear your mind. It is full of absolute lies. All that temptation offers is condemnation." Brytesworth grasped Jasper's shoulders. Her fingers curled around his him. "Let it drift away."

Jasper stared down at the ground. His eyes followed the gentle swirling lights of the Colni flowers now wading through the earth in gentle spirals. The heart of the forest still pounded in his ears but he focused on ignoring it and forced a deep breath. The vibrant orange fruit vividly grew in Jasper's mind; he tried pushing it out of his consciousness.

Jasper could feel Brytesworth's gaze soften as she watched him meditate. A warm and callous hand pressed against his shoulder. He felt Brytesworth massage his arm.

"We have lost a day trekking back here but we should be able to make it back to the first opening and camp again fairly easily if we leave now. Thankfully you made it all the way back. We have another three days." Brytesworth began to walk back towards McMichaels.

Jasper felt the foreign pulse shoot through his feet and jolt up his spine, now louder than ever. Jasper groaned and rolled to his feet. It felt like the next step in evolution. He could already feel himself transforming.

Brytesworth turned back to face Jasper when she was halfway between him and McMichaels. "Jasper?" she asked in a suspicious tone.

The gentle swirls of light in the earth straightened into harsh beams once again. They swung around the barrier viciously. McMichaels ducked; Brytesworth was struck as she attempted to chase down Jasper.

Jasper leapt through the barrier and blindly sprinted up hill. The trees were less than a foot apart; Jasper side shuffled between them using the vibrations from the tree as his only guide. "I must have it," he muttered to himself. A tingling sensation consumed his limbs and renewed his strength. Jasper felt like he had enough energy to sprint around the world three times.

He felt his foot touch a root extending from the heart. The sound of the tree was almost deafening and Jasper could hear his name in the rhythm of its pulse.

The world danced in his open palm like a top spinning on a hard wood floor. Jasper could see himself sitting on top of the clouds, within a stone's throw of eternity. He could list off the stars more easily than letters in the alphabet. All of these possibilities were now less than three feet away.

A dim orange glow illuminated out of the corner of his eye. He turned; the closer he inched towards it, the brighter it became. He was able to make out the deep details of the trunk. Its roots surrounded the tree like a spider web. A small swarm of ants marched around the tree and looked like a flood of black water. They parted before Jasper stepped down, and continued to split with his every step.

The orange glow was less than a foot above his head. His mouth watered, but his mind rumbled louder than his stomach.

A great deal of weight dropped on to Jasper as he tried to reach for the fruit. Nothing held him back; there was nothing even near him. He tried to shake the pressure off but it wrapped even more tightly around his body. Like a snake it slithered around his torso and constricted. Jasper could feel his ribs about to crack as he tried to smuggle air into his lungs like contraband.

The light was beginning to escape; Jasper was being consumed by the darkness surrounding him. He tried to fight the tunnel from shrinking but it steadily continued to compress.

Out of desperation he summoned all of his energy and bashed his body against the tree. The grip slightly loosened. Jasper attempted the strike again and once more the grip loosened. The light from the tree was beginning to fight back and as it did the unknown force diminished.

Jasper regained his breath in moments and eagerly looked up at the now vibrant orange glow. He reached to claim his prize, but when he was only inches away a loud footstep crashed against the ground, no more than perhaps ten feet away. Jasper could feel the heartbeat from the root of the tree quicken, a terrified drumroll. After the second thud Jasper's pulse matched the tree's. He surveyed the surrounding area as best he could.

He saw Brytesworth and McMichaels return to borders of the light barrier and huddle within the Colni patch. Whatever was marching towards them was so close that Jasper could hear its breathing. He could hear it dragging something and imagined a giant monster carrying a tree as a club.

He looked back up at the vague outline of the fruit, it had retreated almost six feet higher. Jasper reached for the lowest branch but it was too far for him to even brush against. Another loud thud crashed.

Jasper glimpsed over his shoulder, but it was no use. He could not see a foot past the trunk. "Protect me," Jasper pleaded and jumped towards the trunk. He kicked against it and leapt for the branch. As he gripped it with both hands, the tree vibrated. Pulling himself up on the branch, so he could rest his back against the tree, he looked up and saw he was less than a foot away from the fruit. Jasper cupped what felt like an apple in his hands; though he did not remove it from the branch. It was warm to the touch. It was like a small sun bringing life to Jasper and everything surrounding it.

He could feel a chest full of secrets hiding inside the fruit, waiting to be opened. As Jasper began to twist the fruit from the tree, the earth shook so violently that Jasper lost his footing and fell to the ground. A root jabbed into his back and stirred a wave of nausea. He rolled over, in immense pain, and dry heaved. The smell of his own illness made him dizzy. Something crunched, high above the ground. Debris from the branches over him crumbled to the ground.

The sound of the beast's breathing was almost drowned out by hisses of snakes that Jasper could almost feel sliding out of the darkness. He tightened every muscle in his body as he waited for his attacker to strike. He was paralyzed in fear and could hear them inching closer.

Rather than swarm, they circled. Jasper could hear them dancing through the darkness, keeping their distance. He remembered Brytesworth's story about falling into complete emptiness and began to sob.

From under the earth he felt a mouth widen. His feet dangled over the edge as it spread and wider. He could feel himself slipping deeper inside. Any moment he would have nothing to lean on and would fall into the abyss.

Unable to breath, Jasper clawed at his throat and

chest. But his body fought back and his limbs went numb. He felt himself tipping into the never ending darkness, the ground stopped shaking. The deafening hissing died down to almost a complete silence. And in the distance Jasper could see a glowing grey light. It looked as if it were hovering towards him; but as the light came nearer Jasper could see it was a humanoid figure.

"Zimriah?" Jasper mouthed the name, too scared to actually speak.

"I had such hope for you," Zimriah replied in his stoic tone. "But you all are the same virus."

"I didn't mean to--"

"It was the only thing you meant to do. And not only did you mean to do it, but you wanted to."

"Please," Jasper sniffled. He choked down his mucus wiped away his dripping saliva. "Please forgive me." His voice cracked when he finished.

"This is forgiveness. Forgiveness is through punishment."

"But I didn't even..." Jasper trailed off. He was about to say he did not even attack the tree. He wasn't given the chance.

Zimriah raised his forehead, where his eyebrows would be. "You betrayed us."

There was a moment of silence. Jasper finally

controlled his breathing before responding. "I'm sorry. To be honest, I don't even know if I would have been able to stop. For a while I could hear nothing except my name coming from its beat. It felt as if it were literally calling me no matter how far I ran."

"It called to you?"

"Even in my sleep. I was excited to leave this place and explore the other side but I woke up only feet from the Colni patch. I thought it was just a dream at first, but it just felt so real."

"It is a powerful part of our existence. It does not mean to attract attention, but everything within our walls relies on it in order to exist. Even breathing in its general vicinity can cause a disturbance. A mere touch could paralyze half of the forest or destroy it beyond repair."

"I just..." Jasper wiped his face. "I just wish I could take it back. Or show you how sorry I am."

"That is why you must be punished. To prove it."

Jasper looked away. He forced a swallow but it stung his throat. Zimriah now stood mere inches away. Jasper hunched his shoulders. "I understand," his voice shook. Zimriah pulled on the wall of the void and led them back to the forest. He walked over to the tree to investigate any damage that Jasper had caused.

It was no longer pitch black. Jasper looked up

and saw the hill that he and McMichaels fell down when they first stumbled upon the Colni patch. It was covered in protruding roots and small rocks. The tree Zimriah inspected stood alone; only a few flowers grew within a five foot radius. But outside that zone everything bundled together. The trees all stood less than a foot apart. Jasper rubbed his arm as he looked at the narrow passage he had to traverse.

Zimriah waved Jasper over. They walked through the light barrier and stood under the dome. Brytesworth and McMichaels were still sitting in the Colni patch. Jasper's body trembled. "What are you doing?" he asked, but Zimriah ignored him and kept walking. Jasper had trouble following. His legs felt like they were melting. He was barely able to drag them along.

"I have reached a decision," Zimriah finally said. It was in the same matter a fact tone he always spoke in, so Jasper could not get any sort of read on what was about to be said. He held his arms in front of his body; his teeth were chattering.

"Your failed attempt to destroy our most sacred life source has deemed you an outlaw to our existence. Therefore you must never set foot in our forest again."

Jasper looked over at McMichaels and Brytesworth, who both appeared to be just as confused as he was. He then turned to Zimriah, who showed no emotion. If anything he looked more like a statue.

"You are permanently exiled from the forest. You, under the penalty of a most painful death, are to never set foot within our boundaries again."

"What?" Jasper half whispered. He perked up and felt his muscles loosen. He forced his mouth shut, scared to say anything that might change the punishment.

"You may exit the forest one of two ways," Zimriah pointed behind him. "You may return to your village and live out the rest of your days there. Or you can finish the path you started and exit the forest into the unknown world. You have one minute to decide and your decision is final."

Jasper looked over at McMichaels, who had always had reservations about leaving his home. He could not tell what his friend was thinking. However, it was not McMichaels' decision to make.

Jasper remembered digging through dry earth and planting seeds outside his house that he knew would never grow. The village did not have many generations left. He would be living with an expiration date. Out of the corner of his eye, he saw McMichaels nod.

"Your time is up," Zimriah said. "What is your decision? And make it quick."

"I, um…"

"Make your decision now."

"Take me to the edge," Jasper blurted out. No one spoke for a moment. Jasper looked over to Brytesworth and McMichaels, who were both fixated on Zimriah.

"Very well," Zimriah said, and he jabbed his open hands into the ground. He looked like he was pulling on a rope beneath the earth's surface. Jasper heard what sounded like a rock splitting in two. He turned around and saw the earth rippling together like someone was pulling a loose thread from the waste of a pair of pants.

In the distance Jasper could see a small light. It grew and came closer. Before long Jasper could see that it was an exit to the forest and Zimriah was pulling it closer.

"Never return," Zimriah said when the exit to the forest was only feet away.

Jasper nodded and took the first two steps towards the exit. There was a harsh white light coming from the distance, in between two mountains. At first Jasper needed to use his hand like a visor and cover his face, but as his eyes adjusted he was able to see in the near distance, what looked like a small collection of cabins. Some of them even looked similar to the inner village houses.

"Are you ready for this?" McMichaels patted Jasper on the shoulder, half to encourage him, half to physically push him to safety.

"Uh huh." Jasper was in awe. He looked out at the black roads covered in white and yellow lines. "This is, wow." He turned back to Brytesworth. "Are you coming?" Jasper asked. He made sure to continue walking towards to threshold as he spoke.

"I've already found my home. I wish you two the best of luck," she replied.

Jasper wanted to ask her more but he caught Zimriah's eye and continued his walk. He jumped through the opening dividing the forest from the light.

A gust of wind greeted him and nearly took him off his feet. It kicked a mouthful of dust into his face. He broke out in laughter and waved the cloud of dirt away. McMichaels helped Jasper back to his feet. They stood on top of a round, grassy hill.

"So, should we check out those houses?" McMichaels pointed to the small town on the other end of the road, at the bottom of the hill.

Jasper took one last glance at the forest. It was near unrecognizable; the daunting, sharp trees almost looked innocent. They stood quietly at their edge; they almost looked asleep. Jasper turned back around and looked down the hill. "I think we should just see it all."

R.K. Gold is an internationally published poet and novelist from Buffalo, NY. He graduated from the University of Maryland with a Bachelor's degree in English and Literature and has appeared in over a dozen publications since he began seriously pursuing writing in January 2014.

His influences range from traditional American writers and poets like Ernest Hemingway, Langston Hughes, and Kurt Vonnegut, to pop icons like Alan Moore, Stan Lee, and Stephen King.

A writer, an environmentalist, and a dog lover, R.K. Gold hopes to make novels and philanthropy his full time profession in the future.

If you are interested in contacted him you can reach him at rkgold91@gmail.com

A list of his publications can be found on his website http://www.rkgoldcreations.com/publications.html

You can like his fan page at

www.facebook.com/rkgoldcreations

And follow him on twitter @RKGold91

Other Titles From Weasel Press

http://weaselpress.storenvy.com

Viscera by Manna Plourde: A story that focuses on Miranda, a female protagonist who is quiet in the face of her own suffering, the threat of masculinity, the juxtaposition of violence and sexuality. ISBN-13: 978-0692365946

Wolf: An Epic and Other Poems by Z.M. Wise: The author's spirit animal bares all teeth in this epic, along with ten other wolf/werewolf-themed poems. As always, Mr. Wise proudly proclaims, "POETRY LIVES!!" ISBN-13: 978-0692370520

Improbable...Never Impossible by Vixyy Fox: You are invited into one of the finest collections a writer has to offer. We have a baker's dozen plus a few extra tales to spur one's imagination; stories that will give you laughter, and maybe even some tears in your journey. ISBN-13: 978-0692342503

In Another Life, Maybe by Michael Prihoda: This Chabook charts the collapse of a romantic relationship, though it treats its subject in nonlinear ways, and deals with the anxiety, pain, stress, and the misunderstanding inherent to any relationship's demise. ISBN-13: 978-0692418864

Tales in Liquid Time by Neil S. Reddy: We bring our dear readers 11 shocking and strange tales of fiction with a bit of harsh bluesy charm and wit. Step into this other world of weird concoctions, wander through these ravishing page pages of true science fiction! ISBN-13: 978-0692297179

Ideological Pandemonium by Szabo Eduard Drago-mir: The aim of this chapbook is the delivery of a mockery at the wrongly formed notion of "equality" that some individuals have, emphasizing on the fact that vile shadows cannot be destroyed without destroying the pure objects that propagate them while also demonstrating that a wrongful grasp of a certain notion can lead to calumnious aftermaths. ISBN-13: 978-0692334171

Inevitable by Amy L. Sasser: Poetry is an anarchist's art, and when the muses plague us the creations that appear after their call are inevitable. This collection is simply the powerful aftermath from the destructive plague the muses bring in. ISBN-13: 978-0692314586

The Madness of Empty Spaces by David E. Cowen: There is a few select working and living in the darker forms of poetry, those who spew out the daunting and sometimes horrific subjects the world around us has to offer. The Madness of Empty Spaces is a celebration of the macabre. ISBN-13: 978-0692332962

Paradise Hills by Kai Neidhardt: This collection is a gritty and grungy exploration of life through intense poetry and energetic words. ISBN-13: 978-0692359846

H a i l by Stanford Cheung: From the industrial eccentricity of inner undulation, to the experimental approach of progressive musicology, the poems in HAIL speak of the psychological depictions of interpretation and musical ethnocentrism. ISBN-13: 978-0692421321

Thunder In My Home by C. Lynn Carden AKA Happy Daze Poet: Take an emotional ride with 25 poems mixed with images to focus on the startling effects of domestic abuse. This isn't mere glamorizing or profit for profit's sake. This collection is here to help those who need it; to awaken readers and help spread awareness to a growing problem today. ISBN-13: 978-0692303948

Exist in the Moon by Jessi Schultz: First time release for
this poet, this chapbook is an acheivement of inner balance through
meditative poetry. ISBN-13: 978-0692254448